Sarah H. Foster

The Portsmouth Guide Book

comprising a survey of the city and neighborhood, with notices of the principal

buildings, sites of historical interest, and public institutions

Sarah H. Foster

The Portsmouth Guide Book
comprising a survey of the city and neighborhood, with notices of the principal buildings, sites of historical interest, and public institutions

ISBN/EAN: 9783337368166

Printed in Europe, USA, Canada, Australia, Japan

Cover: Foto ©Andreas Hilbeck / pixelio.de

More available books at **www.hansebooks.com**

THE

Portsmouth Guide Book:

COMPRISING

A Survey of the City and Neighborhood,

WITH NOTICES OF THE

PRINCIPAL BUILDINGS, SITES OF HISTORICAL INTEREST AND PUBLIC INSTITUTIONS.

———◆———

"Walk about Zion, and go round about her ; tell the towers thereof. Mark ye well her bulwarks, consider her palaces ; that ye may tell it to the generation following."

———

To us who walk in summer
Through the cool and sea-blown town,
From the childhood of its people
Comes the solemn legend down.

—*Whittier.*

———◆———

PORTSMOUTH
JOSEPH H. FOSTER.
1876.

PREFACE.

The increasing number of summer visitors to our "City by the Sea," and its picturesque neighborhood, has made the want of a Portsmouth Guide Book much felt; while the great interest at present pervading the country, in all historical memorials, has turned the attention of many persons to our old landmarks. The little book now offered to the public is intended to meet the wants of both these classes, and yet to be so brief and inexpensive as to come into the hands of all.

The claims of Portsmouth to the notice of antiquarians are scarcely inferior to those of any city in our Union; and its Revolutionary record stands so high, that it well deserves more thorough research than is possible in so small a volume as the present.

The plan is taken from some European guidebooks; the city being divided into convenient walks, in the course of which mention is made of all the places of interest; and at the close of the walk a concise history of each is given. Attention has been mainly directed to the old houses yet standing, and to some of those now demolished, whose site is still known; and a brief history of such has been presented, as far as the writer has been able to ascertain it. The chief sources from which historical information has been drawn, are the collection of Provincial Papers of New Hampshire, the "Annals of Portsmouth" by Nathaniel Adams, now entirely out of print, and the two volumes of "Rambles About Portsmouth," by Chas. W. Brewster, a work too well known to need praise here, and in which the reader will find more extensive information on these subjects than this volume can contain.

The walks are not extended beyond the town itself. Of the places of interest in the neighborhood, which are enumerated at the close, no exhaustive account has been attempted. Many places both in the city and its immediate vicinity have doubtless been omitted, which deserve notice, and mistakes will probably be found; but any corrections, and any interesting information, will be gratefully received, and will be used in the next edition.

MARCH, 1876.　　　　　　　　　　　　　S. H. F.

Walk First.

Pleasant Street, and the part of the city below the South Mill Bridge.

For practical purposes, Market Square is considered as the centre of the City of Portsmouth, and at this centre our walks will commence. If you leave it in a south-easterly direction, you go down Pleasant street, toward the South End. Notice first the high roofed house* next to the North Church, and then the handsome Custom-house* and Post Office. On your left are the Exchange Buildings, containing offices and stores. Crossing State street you pass the residence of the late Hon. Richard Jenness*; and then, crossing Court street, you enter on the original Pleasant* street, thickly peopled with old memories. Mr. Call's house, on the left hand, has but recently taken the place of Deacon Penhallow's house,* while opposite, next to the corner house, is the old Parsonage,* and adjoining it, the residence of the late John K. Pickering*, both sites being of interest. Then comes the celebrated Gov. Langdon house,* and the house and grounds of Mark H. Wentworth;*

while opposite is the Universalist church,* with a view of the South Pond, which is simply an inlet from the sea, and not a fresh pond. Next to the field called Rogers field, stands the Tibbetts House,* and opposite is Brimstone hill.* Next to it stand the house of the late Joseph Haven* and the ancient-looking dwelling at the corner of Gates street; on the right hand the Parry house*, the mansion of Dr. Samuel Haven*, and pretty little Livermore* street, containing but three houses, but all of interest. At the corner of Livermore street is a church* altered into three tenements. Then you pass the Pleasant street cemetery,* and the head of Washington street. At the corner of Wentworth street stands the residence of the late Eben Wentworth*, beyond which you pass old houses, but none of historic note, until you reach the South Mill Bridge.*

Crossing the bridge you observe a green triangular space, where stood of old the first Puritan meeting house* in Portsmouth. Keeping to the right hand down South street, you pass the Haven school house* with the Arsenal* adjoining, and go on among venerable looking houses which no doubt have stories of interest connected with them, if they could but find words to utter them. No. 19* certainly has, and No. 27, the Gardiner House.*

After a pleasant walk of half a mile, you come to the Cotton* cemetery, adjoining which lie the Proprietors'* and the Harmony Grove* Cemeteries. If

you keep to the left, round the corner of the cemeteries, you are on the road to Little Harbor and Sagamore Creek; on the right hand, Richards Avenue or
Miller Avenue would lead you back to the city,
while the direct road goes over Lincoln Hill toward
Greenland.

If, after crossing the Mill Bridge, you keep to the
left, down Water street, you pass the Henry P. Salter
house, built before the Revolution, and then go
through an ancient and dilapidated suburb, past
three or four lanes leading down to the water, and
soon find yourself on a curving road along the border
of the harbor, looking across to Peirce's Island and
to Kittery beyond it. The tide once flowed up here
full and high, but it is now choked with grass and
mud. A few minutes' walk brings you to the Point,
so called, and to the toll bridge to Newcastle. The
same place can be reached from South street, by a
lane called Newcastle street.

Building behind North Church.

Erected in 1800, by Daniel Austin; the first three
story store ever built in Portsmouth. At that time
there were only fifteen three story houses in town,
and most of them built within five years. In this
building Col. Joshua Wentworth had his place of business. (*See Johnson house.*) The high roof was
added later. Before this house was built, the one
which now forms No. 2 Court street, (q. v.) stood here.

Custom House and Post Office.

Erected by the United States in 1858, on the site formerly occupied by the Rockingham Bank, and the hotel called the Piscataqua House. The Custom house and Post office previously in use for fifty years (except for a short interval,) was on the corner of Penhallow and Daniel streets. Still earlier, the Custom house was at Col. Whipple's office, 91 State street. The Post Office was kept in a store on Buck street till 1805; then in a house on Haymarket square. For the first Custom house and Post office, see "*Stone store.*"

House of Hon. Richard Jenness.

Built by the widow of Robert Treadwell in 1818. It stands on the site of the house where the Packer family lived in 1735, and we know not how much earlier. The stone wall on Court street running as far as the engine house, remains as it was in their time. Here lived Sheriff Packer, when in 1768 he hung Ruth Blay (*see Cemeteries*); and in front of this house the mob set up the effigy.

The house was afterwards occupied by Col. Brewster as a boarding house, and here Washington was quartered during his visit to Portsmouth in 1789. The building was burnt in the fire of 1813.

Pleasant Street.

In 1673, Capt. John Pickering 2d, gave to the town a highway two rods wide, through his land, to the milldam. The Dock, now called Puddle Dock, came far up into the land at that time, and the tide sometimes flowed across to the South Pond. The principal part of the land below this division, forming what is now called the South End, belonged to Capt. Pickering, and was called Pickering's Neck.

The northern portion of what is now called Pleasant street was formerly called Court street, from the old Court House then on Market Square.

Deacon Penhallow's House.

The house which stood at the S. E. corner of Court street, and which now forms No. 12 Washington street, was the residence of Deacon Samuel Penhallow, justice of the peace; a man of much note and influence in his day. Rev. Dr. Buckminster boarded here when he commenced his ministry in 1779. The house and its occupants are graphically described in Mrs. Lee's Memoir of Dr. Buckminster. Here, Hon. John Sullivan, afterwards General and President of N. H., pleaded his first cause.

Old Parsonage.

Built by the North Parish in 1792 as a parsonage, and used as such for above forty years. Dr. Buckminster was its first occupant. The glebe land beyond the Creek was leased for the first time, in order to raise funds for its erection. (*See Glebe land.*)

House of late J. K. Pickering.

Built about 1770 by Hopestill March of Dover, a

mulatto, and first occupied by Rev. Dr. Samuel Langdon. Dr. Langdon was born in Boston in 1722, and settled over the North Church in Portsmouth in 1747. In 1774 he was chosen President of Harvard College, and resigned his ministry here. He was a zealous patriot and excellent pastor.

The roof of this house, made with a double pitch, is called a gambrel roof. As this is the first gambrel roof that we have seen, it is well to say that the roof of a house often designates its age, at least within fifty years. The oldest houses have steep roofs; the gambrels came into fashion about 1730, and went out after the Revolution, when large square houses with flat roofs became the rage. Of course many roofs vary from these types.

On the site of this house stood the first parsonage in Portsmouth, and adjoining it, the first place of worship, an Episcopal chapel; both erected prior to 1638, though the exact date is unknown. Rev. Richard Gibson was the first clergyman. The plate and service books for the chapel were sent over by Mason, one of the founders of the colony.

Gov. Langdon's House.

Built by Gov. Langdon in 1784, and occupied by him until his death in 1819. John Langdon, a grandson of Tobias Langdon, (see *Elwyn farm*,) was born in 1739. With the rest of his family, he was an earnest patriot. He was engaged with Capt. Pickering in seizing the powder from the Fort, (*see Fort Constitution*,) which his cousin, Samuel Langdon, afterwards carried to the army at Cambridge; this same cousin, in Feb. 1778, conducted two teams loaded with clothing to Valley Forge, a gift from Portsmouth to Washington's suffering army. John Langdon filled many offices, civil and military, and in 1805 was elected Governor of New Hampshire. When Louis Philippe and his brothers were here in 1780, they found no room at the Stavers Hotel, and were hospitably received at this house. In after years, when on the throne of France, Louis inquired of a Portsmouth lady presented at his court, whether the Gov. Langdon mansion was still in existence. Washington regarded it as the handsomest house in Portsmouth.

It was afterwards owned by Rev. Dr. Burroughs, who for forty-five years was rector of St. John's church, and is still the residence of his widow. The house, as well as the extensive grounds, are kept in beautiful preservation. The small brick lodges in front seem built to guard the entrance.

Mark H. Wentworth's House.

Built by Capt. Thomas Thompson in 1784. Capt. Thompson was one of the first naval officers commissioned by the Continental Congress. He commanded the frigate Raleigh, (*see Islands in Harbor*); and afterwards (1785) was colonel of a Regiment of Artillery. The house was long the residence of Dr.

Josiah Dwight, who married a daughter of Capt.
Thompson. A large and ancient elm stands on the
premises.

The spot where the barn stands was previously occupied by a Sandemanian meeting house, built in
1764, when Mr. Sandeman first promulgated his ten-
ets. When this house was built by Capt. Thompson,
the meeting house was taken down, and the society
afterwards worshipped in a room in the brick school-
house on State street. Jonathan M. Sewall, the poet,
was a member of this church. The society is now
extinct, as the sect probably is.

Universalist Church.

Built in 1808. The Universalist Society was incorporated in 1793. Their first meeting house was
on Vaughan street. (*See Cameneum.*)

Tibbetts House.

The earliest notice we have of this house is of its
sale in 1774 by Thomas Jackson, to Dr. Daniel
Peirce of Kittery. It is described as situated on the
street "leading by Dr. Samuel Haven's dwelling house
to the mill dam, and next to the land of Daniel Rogers"—(still called Rogers' field.) In 1791, when it was
sold to Richard Salter Tibbetts, the street is called
Pleasant Street.

Brimstone Hill.

This slight elevation of land, with its portentous
name, was for generations a play spot for boys, and

the scene of coasting frolics without end. It has recently been spoiled for such purposes by buildings.

The origin of its name is doubtful. Some ascribe it to the former saltpetre manufactory opposite; while some put faith in a tradition that Daniel Fowle lived in the old Smith House on the summit, and united to his business of printing, that of making roll-brimstone—a Yankee Dr. Faustus.

Joseph Haven's House.

Built in 1780 by Joseph Haven, son of Rev. Samuel Haven, and occupied by him till his death in 1829. This was the site where the southern portion of the town wished to have the new church built, at the time of the division of the parishes. (*See North Church.*)

All that is known of the much more ancient building at the corner of Gates street is, that it formerly stood on the site of this house, with its end to the street. It was removed to its present position when Mr. Haven built his house.

Parry House.

At the time of the Revolution this lot was vacant, and was used by Dr. Haven, who lived close by, as a place for the manufacture of saltpetre for the army.

The present house was soon afterwards built by Edward Parry, whose name was then of note as a prominent merchant. To him were consigned the cargoes of tea, in 1774, which caused almost as much excitement as did the tea ships in Boston; but whatever he received he promptly reshipped untouched.

Mr. Parry was from Wales. When he built this house he constructed a small fort on the border of the South Pond, and mounted there a brass cannon and a flag. This fort he named Fort Anglesea, and it stood for many years.

Dr. Samuel Haven's House.

Built about 1760 by Dr. Haven, who was pastor of the South Parish from 1762 to 1803. Dr. Haven was born in Framingham, Mass., in 1727. He was a warm patriot and exemplary pastor. He died in 1806, his wife dying a few hours after him.

Livermore Street and House.

The house now occupied by Albert R. Hatch was built about 1730 by Matthew Livermore, who was born in 1703 and came here in 1724 to teach school. He became an eminent lawyer, and was appointed King's Advocate and Attorney General of the Province of New Hampshire. He died here in 1776. His relative, Samuel Livermore, who also lived here, was a distinguished man in his time, and chief adviser of Gov. Wentworth. At the time this house was built, it faced Pleasant street, having an open yard in front. More than fifty years later, Livermore street was opened, and the house moved to its present position.

The three-story brick house which stands opposite,

was the home of Dr. Nathan Parker, the honored and beloved pastor of the South Parish for twenty-three years, until his death in 1833.

The small, wooden house beside it, was that in which the first Sunday school in Portsmouth, and almost the first in the country, was collected in June 1818. It then stood on Wentworth street, being used as a lecture room by the South Parish, under Dr. Parker's ministry. The Sunday school met here until 1828, when it removed to Court St. (*See Unitarian Chapel.*) This building was then brought here, and used as a vestry by the church adjoining; and was afterwards altered into a dwelling house by the addition of a second story.

Pleasant Street Church.

Built for a Congregational Church in 1829 by a branch of the North Church. It was afterwards sold to the Christian Baptists, and finally altered into dwelling houses in 1858.

Pleasant Street Cemetery.

This spot was deeded to the town for a burial place by Capt. John Pickering in 1754. It is now disused and closed. The oldest headstones in it are those of two children of Dr. Samuel Haven, dated 1761. There are other stones with the dates of 1763, 4 & 5, but none of historic interest.

Eben. Wentworth House.

Built about 1769 for the last Governor John Went-

worth, son of Mark Hunking and nephew of Benning
(*see Little Harbor*). He was born in 1736, and received his commission as Governor in 1766. When
the Revolution begun, he was still the Royal Governor
and therefore felt that his duty compelled him to take
the king's side, at the same time that his father and uncle were active in the cause of liberty. In 1775, it
being known that an obnoxious royalist named Fenton
had taken refuge in the governor's house, a mob
gathered before it, demanding that he should be giv-
en up. This was done, and the governor left the
house to seek protection at Fort William and Mary,
while the mob entered the house and ransacked the
premises. A broken marble chimney piece is preserved as a memento of the attack. Gov. Wentworth
afterwards went to England, and never returned to
New Hampshire ; but was created Baronet and appointed Governor of Nova Scotia, (1792,) where he
died in 1820. He was very fond of horses, and the
large stable which stood nearly opposite until recently, was his stable, in which he kept sixteen horses
for his own use.

South Mill and Bridge.

In 1658, the town granted this mill privilege to the
first John Pickering, who came to Portsmouth in
1636, and from whom all the families of the name in
the neighborhood are descended.

The grant was made upon condition of his keeping
in repair a road over the dam for foot passengers

going to church. The bridge at first was but six feet wide. Mr. Pickering built the mill at the same time. The property remained in the family until about 1790.

First Puritan Meeting House.

In 1658 a meeting house was built upon the hill below the milldam; the only place of worship previously erected having been the Episcopal chapel on Pleasant street.

The house was of two stories, with a low belfry, in which, in 1664, was hung the first bell used in New Hampshire. It had at first neither pews nor window shutters. Rev. Joshua Moody was the first minister. He began to preach at once, but was not regularly ordained until 1671.

The building was used until the erection of the Old South, in 1731. Soon after, the old church was taken to pieces, a part being used to enlarge the schoolhouse near by, while part was moved to King street, and converted into a dwelling house. (*See Congress Block.*)

Haven School House.

Built in 1846. It contains four graded schools; infant, primary, intermediate and grammar.

Nearly on the same site, was built, in 1709, the first public school-house in Portsmouth. Eight years earlier the widow Graffort had left to the town a lot of land on Daniel street, to be used for the site of a schoolhouse, but it had never been used for the purpose. The first record that we have of any action on the subject of schools is in 1697, when Thomas Phipps was appointed schoolmaster by the town. He filled this office for several years, a small building on the site of the brick schoolhouse on State st. being hired for his use, from the Wentworth family.

In 1708 the Assembly ordered that a free Province school be established in Portsmouth, for "righters, reeders, and Latiners." In consequence of this decree, the selectmen ordered that "Capt. John Pickering tack care and agre with Left. Pears for erecting a school house on ye south sd of ye mill dam," &c.—which was done.

In 1732 the school house was enlarged by the addition of a portion of the old meeting house, and the bell was transferred to it. It stood until 1846, when the present structure took its place.

State Arsenal.

The land on which this arsenal is built, was appropriated by the town to the State in 1808, and the building was erected to hold ammunition and artillery belonging to government. The arsenal is now disused.

Until within a few years, two brass field pieces have been kept here, which were brought from Louisberg by Sir William Pepperrell. Unfortunately they were sent to Claremont, where they were melted down.

No. 19---Dr. Mitchell's House.

When this old house was built is not known, but about 1750 it was occupied by Dr. Mitchell, whose daughter Lettice was one of the beauties of the town. She was engaged to be married to a son of Daniel Warner, (*see Buckminster House,*) but during his absence in Europe, in 1759, she was persuaded to marry the King's attorney, Wyseman Clagett, and went to live an unhappy life in his house on King st. (*See Leavitt house.*) Her first lover died of a broken heart after his return.

Gardiner House.

The date of erection of this house is unknown, but it is very old. In 1768 it was purchased from a Mr. Noland by Peter Shores, the ancestor of all the families of that name in Portsmouth. Mr. Shores' daughter married Samuel Gardiner, a brother of Major Gardiner, who came and lived here. The house has remained in the family, and has never been altered except by the removal of the large window shutters from the lower story.

Cotton's Burying Ground.

In 1671 the town agreed with Goodman William Cotton to clear and fence the land now occupied by this cemetery and the one adjoining it. He was to have the use of it for twenty years as a pasture, and after that it was to be a training field and a burial place. In 1721 the burying ground now called Cotton's was enclosed separately, the rest being used as a training field.

There are many ancient gravestones here, but for the most part they are so defaced by time as to be illegible. The Rev. John Emerson was interred here in 1732, but his remains have been removed to the adjoining cemetery. The oldest legible stones are those of Walter Clarkson, 1739, Samuel Shortridge, 1759, and Elizabeth Hall, 1762. An interesting monument is standing to Charles Chauncey, son of Dr. Chauncey of Boston and nephew of Sir Wm. Pepperrell, who died in 1809, aged 81.

Proprietors' Burying Ground.

This was the training field spoken of above. It was here that Capt. John Pickering first trained his Puritan company. In 1735 the town gave the use of it to Rev. Mr. Shurtleff for a pasture; and this privilege was afterward extended to every minister of the South Parish. When the training field at the Plains began to be used, this was left for a pasture only, and called the Minister's field. When the Stone Church was built, the property was transferred to the Trustees of the Charity Fund, who in 1830 laid out here the "Proprietors' Burying Ground," so called as being the first Cemetery other than the public ones.

Harmony Grove Cemetery was laid out in 1847, and a still further addition, called "Sagamore Cemetery," in 1871. When Green street Cemetery (q. v.) was demolished in 1875, the remains found there, including those of President Cutt's family, were carefully removed hither, and the old stones set up in a prominent situation in the yard.

On the highest part of the ground, in the Proprietors' Burying Ground, near the pond, was hung in Aug. 1768, a girl named Ruth Blay, for the supposed murder of an illegitimate child. Extenuating circumstances having come to light, a reprieve was obtained from the Governor, to be followed probably by a pardon. The reprieve would have arrived in time, but that Sheriff Packer, fearing to be late for dinner, had hurried the execution before the appointed hour. The indignant populace surrounded his house in the evening, and set up an effigy with an insulting inscription. This was the last execution in Portsmouth.

Walk Second.

Water and Washington Streets.

If, on reaching the South Mill Bridge, instead of crossing it, you turn sharply to the left and go up Water street, you will pass through the oldest part of the town.

At the very entrance of the street, you pass a three-story house, the Morrill house;* then you observe some narrow old lanes leading down to the water, on your right. These narrow lanes were once aristocratic places. The second of them, Hunking street, conducts you by the Lear or Storer house;* the next one, Gardiner street, leads to the Gardiner house;* both of them stately mansions in their day. The walk beside the old rotting wharves and the ancient houses, mostly nameless, is well worth taking. Across the entrance to Gardiner street formerly stood the Arch; an arched passage beneath an old dwelling·house. On the opposite side of Water street, on a ·little elevation, stands the South Ward Room, unworthily filling the place of the old South Church.* On one of the narrow cross streets that surround it, notice the old Fernald house,* whose owner, were he living, could tell many a tale of the neighborhood. Passing on, you see to your right Mechanic street, which leads to the Point of Graves,* and to other deserted wharves; while on your left stands the handsome Manning house,* and fronting you, at the end of the short Manning street, the venerable Vaughan house, the first Wentworth house*—its old offices extending down to the water. You now reach Liberty Bridge,* crossing the Dock,* now, alas ! Puddle Dock, but beautiful and commodious once. Beyond the bridge the only site of interest is that of the Great House,* which stood at the south-easterly corner of Court street. Old houses there are, but they have no voices to tell what they were once, and the street is chiefly given up to low shops.

Washington street runs parallel with Water street. To go through it, you turn off from Pleasant street, opposite Gov. Wentworth's. The obliquely built house at the right hand corner was that in which Daniel Fowle* published the first newspaper in New Hampshire. You soon cross the muddy gully where Canoe Bridge* once spanned the Dock, when boats could go up as far as Pleasant street. Old houses surround you; one of them, No. 12, is Deacon Penhallow's house, removed from Pleasant street. The low, yellow house, No. 10, was the residence of Brackett Hutchings, in whose parlor the Methodists

first met for worship, and where their society was
organized. Opposite stand the Salter and Cushman
houses*; while all we know of the forlorn old house
next them is, that in 1791 its owner rejoiced in the
name of Nathaniel Babb. On one corner of Court
street stands the handsome Chase house, more than
150 years old, and still in the family that built it; while
the opposite corner is Dr. Hall Jackson's house.*
Washington street soon terminates in State street.
its own name, as well as the names of the contiguous
streets, show the patriotism of the neighborhood in
Revolutionary times. Liberty, Gates, Hancock, Jefferson,—all obscure streets now, though occasionally
a dwelling can be identified with the past. In No. 5
Gates street lived Jonathan M. Sewall, our Revolutionary poet, who died in 1808; and no doubt other
houses have histories of their own, but the localities
are not especially inviting.

Morrill House.

This house stands on the site of the dwelling of
Capt. Thomas Pickering, one of the most renowned
of our local Revolutionary heroes. He, with a few
like himself, surprised and captured Fort William &
Mary at Newcastle, Dec. 15, 1774, (*see Fort Constitution,*) securing for the patriots the powder and
small arms, and for themselves the honor of making
the first seizure of British property in the war.

In 1775 the Scarborough man-of-war was in our

harbor, causing much annoyance to the inhabitants. Thomas Pickering and Samuel Hutchings went down to Union wharf—the wharf next to Liberty Bridge—and fired upon a provision barge belonging to the ship. The men, in alarm, ran the boat ashore by the Mill Bridge, and abandoned it. Pickering fastened horses to it, and dragged it through the streets to the Pound, where it was locked up.

In October of the same year he and his men boarded and took the British ship Prince George, which came into the harbor in a storm. Nearly 2000 barrels of flour were on board, which were sent to Washington's army in Cambridge; 300 barrels being reserved, with Washington's consent, for the use of Portsmouth; as "for weeks there had not been a barrel of flour to be bought in the Province."

Capt. Pickering afterwards had command of the Hampden, a vessel of 20 guns, and was killed in an engagement in 1779. His brother, John, was the owner of the South Mill during the Revolution. The first street running to the right from Water street bears Pickering's name.

Lear House.

The date of the erection of this house is not known; but Tobias Lear was born here in 1760. He was Washington's private secretary for 16 years, until the President's death. In 1789 Washington visited this house, which was then occupied by Mrs. Lear,

the stepmother of the secretary, and by Samuel Storer, whose wife was his sister and mother of the
late Admiral Storer. The room where the distinguished guest was received has never been altered.

Gardiner House.

Built by the Wentworth family, date unknown.
At the time of the Revolution two brothers lived
here, named Nichols, one of whom was the father of
Rev. Dr. Nichols of Portland, who was born here. In
1792 it was purchased of them by Major Wm. Gardiner. Major Gardiner was born in 1751, and was an
eminent patriot, and Commissary for the Revolutionary army, in which office he lost nearly all his property. He died here in 1833.

The house is beautifully finished in the inside.
The splendid linden tree in front is 150 years old,
and measures 12 feet in circumference 10 feet from
the ground.

It was Maj. Gardiner who built the house where
the arch was. The room over the arch was occupied
by him after the war as U. S. loan officer.

South Church.

Until 1712 the only meeting house was the one below the bridge; in that year the North Church was
built, and the town divided into the North and South
Parishes. The latter continued to worship at the old
house under the pastorship of Rev. John Emerson,
until 1731, when the South Church was built.

The land on which the church stood was given by John Pickering, and the timber was cut upon the spot. Mr. Emerson offered a prayer from the staging after the frame was raised, which was the last time he ever spoke in public. He died in the same year, and was succeeded by Rev. William Shurtleff. In 1759 the house was struck by lightning, and the spire torn to pieces, and two or three times afterward it was struck. It is said that Franklin predicted, from its situation, that it would be peculiarly liable to such disasters.

The South Parish occupied this place of worship until 1826, when the Stone Church on State street being finished, they removed thither. It was afterward used temporarily by various societies and schools until 1860, when it was taken down. At that time the remains of two of the former ministers, Rev. Wm. Shurtleff and Rev. Job Strong, were removed from their tombs beneath it, and interred in the Auburn street cemetery, with a suitable monument.

Fernald House.

This ancient looking house was built in 1732 by Samuel Frost. At the time of the Revolution it was owned by Capt. Nichols, father of the late Rev. Dr. Nichols of Portland. In 1788 Capt. Daniel Fernald married a daughter of Capt. Nichols and took the house, where he lived until his death, in 1866, at the age of 98 years.

Point of Graves.

In March 1671, Capt. John Pickering 2d agreed that the town should "have full liberty to enclose about half an acre upon the neck of land on which he liveth, where the people have been wont to be buried, which land shall be impropriated forever unto the use of a burying place." Capt. Pickering's father had previously been buried there.

This old grave yard contains many interesting memorials. The oldest stones now legible bear the names of John Hoddy, 1684; Sarah Redford, 1695; Elizabeth Frost 1696, and two of the Vaughan family, 1690. One of these was Margaret, wife of Wm. Vaughan and daughter of Richard Cutt. Three of the Wentworth family were buried here the same year, but the stone has been renewed. Of somewhat later date are those of a son of Rev. Mr. Rogers, 1704; wife of N. Meserve, 1747; and Tobias Lear, father of the secretary, and his wife, who died in 1781 and 1774. The stone at the entrance bears the date of 1778.

The neighborhood of this old cemetery was once the most active business part of the town; the decaying warehouses were occupied by Jacob Sheafe and others in 1750 and onward. Later, in the war of 1812, when privateering was an important item of Portsmouth enterprise, the old wharf here saw the fitting out of the first privateer, the Nancy, Capt. Smart.

The Manning House.

Formerly the residence of Capt. Thomas Manning, one of the patriots of the Revolution. It was he who changed the name of King street to Congress street, and his name is associated with all the political movements of the time. He was rich and generous, giving freely for all patriotic purposes.

First Wentworth House.

This is probably as old as any house remaining in Portsmouth, except the Jackson house, at Christian Shore, having been built about 1670. The first of the Wentworth name in the town was Samuel, son of Elder William Wentworth of Dover. He was licensed in 1670 to keep a public house and brew beer, and this house was probably built as a public house.

His son, John, afterward Lt. Governor of the province, born in 1671, probably first saw the light here; he certainly lived here at the time of his marriage in 1693; and his son, Benning, afterward Governor, was born here in 1696, as well as fifteen other children, one of whom, Daniel, was the grandfather of the late Eben Wentworth. This was a royal house in its day, and shows its substantial structure yet; its chimney measures 13 feet by 10 at its base, and its beams are 12 by 18 inches. The premises belonging to the house extended from the South Church on one side to the millpond on the other.

It is now owned by Wm. A. Vaughan, a descendant

of Gov. Vaughan, predecessor of Gov. Wentworth. The street now called Manning, was until recently called Wentworth street.

Liberty Bridge.

Built in 1731, and called Swing Bridge, from having a draw to let vessels pass, which Canoe Bridge had not. The name was changed in Jan. 1766, under the following circumstances:

George Meserve, appointed stamp agent for N. H. (*see Meserve House,*) had surrendered his commission upon the demand of a patriotic mob, who carried it through the streets in triumph as far as this bridge, where it was destroyed. They then erected a flagstaff with the motto appended, "Liberty, Property, and No Stamp," and christened the bridge Liberty Bridge. The present flagstaff stands on the same spot as the old one.

Puddle Dock.

The Dock, as it was formerly called, was an inlet from the river of considerable width, and flowed up as far as Pleasant street. It is said that at every high tide the water flowed across this street to the mill-pond, through a gully large enough for boats to pass. A row of stepping stones accommodated foot passengers, while horses sometimes had to wade through two feet of water. The Dock has been gradually narrowed and filled up.

The Great House.

In 1631 John Mason sent over about fifty emigrants to his little colony at Odiorne's Point, (q. v.) one of whom, Humphrey Chadborn, came three miles farther up the river, and built what was called the Great House; the first building of any importance in what is now Portsmouth. It was at the corner of Court and Water streets. The land extending from this point over Church Hill, (where St. John's church now stands,) was covered with strawberry vines, which gave the name of Strawberry Bank to the locality. The farm connected with the Great House covered 1000 acres, of course comprising a large part of the city.

Thomas Warnerton resided in the Great House until 1644; then Sampson Lane for two years, and afterwards Richard Cutt, until his death in 1676. His brother Robert afterward lived here, before he went to Kittery. *(See Whipple Garrison House.)* It remained in the Cutt family until it fell to ruins.

The name of Strawberry Bank was retained until 1653, when, a petition to that effect being presented by the inhabitants, then numbering fifty or sixty families, the township was defined, and the name of Portsmouth given to it. The name was taken from Portsmouth, England, of which town Mason was Governor.

Fowle's Printing Office.

In 1756 Daniel Fowle came to Portsmouth, and

began business as a printer. He had left Boston because of the persecution he had suffered for his political opinions. He immediately began to publish a paper here, the New Hampshire Gazette, which steadily promoted the cause of patriotism. His nephew, Robert Fowle, was associated with him from 1764 to 1774, and the paper was printed with the assistance of an intelligent negro slave named Primus, who was an excellent pressman. It was the first newspaper published in the province, and has never been discontinued unto this day. It is said that this house was built for his· printing office, but was afterwards altered into a dwelling house. Daniel Fowle died in 1787, leaving his business to John Melcher, his apprentice.

Canoe Bridge.

In 1727 the town gave permission to sundry individuals to build a bridge over the cove or Dock (now Puddle Dock) from Wentworth's wharf to Sherburne's wharf, leaving an opening of 25 or 30 feet for the passage of boats or canoes. This was called Canoe bridge. In 1786 Hon. John Langdon rebuilt it and presented it to the town. This was a short time after he had built his house on Pleasant street, and the water from the Dock was conducted into his grounds to form an ornamental pond.

Salter House.

Built by Capt. John Salter in 1770. The deed of conveyance of the land designates it as lying on the street that leads over Canoe bridge ; the land adjoining that of Hon. Theodore Atkinson.

Cushman House.

Built by Capt. Salter in 1791 ; the street being at that time designated as Washington street.

Hon. Samuel Cushman, who lived here, was born in 1783, came to Portsmouth in 1816 and married a daughter of Capt. Salter. He was Representative in Congress from 1835 to 1837, for some years Post Master of the city, and afterwards U. S. Navy Agent, and held many municipal offices. He was a direct descendant of the Robert Cushman who in 1620 was the agent of the Puritan emigrants, and hired the Mayflower for their use ; he followed them the next year, and preached at Plymouth the first New England sermon that was ever printed.

Dr. Hall Jackson's House.

Dr. Hall Jackson, who resided in this house for many years and died here in 1797, was the most eminent physician and surgeon in this part of the country, and had a very extensive practice. During the Revolution he was surgeon in the army, and captain of an artillery corps. His father, Dr. Clement Jackson, who died in 1788, aged 82 years, was almost equally distinguished. Both father and son were much beloved and respected.

Walk Third.

State and Court Streets.

In going down Pleasant street, you cross two
streets at right angles with it — State and Court
streets. To traverse these, we will first turn to the
right, round the corner of the Custom House, into
State, formerly Broad street. This street passes directly through the much controverted "Glebe Land."*
You will see on the left the Stone Church,* and next to
it the home of the late Capt. John McClintock, son of
the Dr. McClintock who was Chaplain of the N. II.
forces at Bunker Hill. Next beyond this stands the
ancient-looking Spence House,* while on the other
side of the street is what remains of the Brackett
house,* No. 83; at the corner of Fleet street is the
Davenport house, and a little beyond, Col. Whipple's
house,* No. 91. You now pass the Rockingham
House,* and crossing Middle street, enter what was
once called Mason street, but which is now a contin-
ation of State street. To the left stands the Calvin
Baptist Church* and vestry; but beyond that, you

see nothing of especial interest, until you ascend Windmill hill,* formerly so called, and see the fine Mason house* and the Catholic church* on Summer street close by. The street continues as far as Cass street, being the longest in town.

If, on leaving Pleasant street, you turn to the left and go down State street to the river, through what was formerly Buck street, and in Colonial times Queen street, you pass among brick houses of comparatively modern origin. The fire of 1813 swept away all this part of the town, as far down as Portsmouth Pier,* and afterwards the erection of wooden houses in the compact part of the town was made a penal offence. It would be interesting to enumerate all the old houses that stood here formerly, but it would demand too much space. We will therefore only call attention to the Episcopal Chapel* on the right, the Brick School-house*, the Methodist Church* and the unpretending Seaman's Home* at No. 8, near the corner of Water street. From the wharf you have a beautiful view of the harbor and Navy Yard.

Court street crosses Pleasant street a little farther down than State. Turning to the right up what was formerly Jaffrey street, you see the Court House* and opposite, on the corner of Fleet street, the old house which contained the first brewery in Portsmouth; and then a long row of stately square mansions, built about the beginning of the century, such as are found frequently in Portsmouth, and one of which Aldrich says every visitor yearns to possess. Conspicuous among them is the house of the late Wm. P. Jones, with its fine garden. Short lanes lead between them to the Pond. On the right side of the street notice the old fashioned flagging stones, the "Durham flat stones," once found in every fashionable street, but now confined almost wholly to this locality and to Washington street. In Alden's century sermon, 1801, he says, " We have but one street entirely paved. In the course of a few years, however, one side of most of our streets has been paved with very nice flat stones brought from Durham, in such a manner that two or three persons can conveniently walk abreast." It is a European style of sidewalk, and so rarely used in this country that it was formerly said that Portsmouth ladies were known by the gait acquired by tripping over such stones as these. The chapel on the right belongs to the Christian Baptist Society. Just as the street terminates in Middle street, notice the mansion of Daniel H. Peirce,* and the old fashioned house opposite, No. 2.*

Turning into Court street from Pleasant street to the left, you come again among old houses, for the fire of 1813 did not extend as far as this, and pass the Unitarian Chapel;* then crossing Washington street, you see an old, three story house on the right, the Stavers Hotel.* On the opposite side of the street is the Underwood House,* and next to it, on the lot now vacant, stood until within a few years one of the finest old buildings in Portsmouth, the Atkinson House.*· No. 45 is the old Bailey house, made immortal by Aldrich as the dwelling place of his Bad Boy. No. 47 is constructed from the old Court House (q. v.) removed hither in 1837.

Glebe Land.

In 1640 the first appointed governor of the colony, Francis Williams, together with the principal inhabitants of Portsmouth, made a grant of 50 acres of land to the town, for glebe or parsonage, and for the support of the ministry. Three-fourths of this land lay at the head of "Strawberry Bank Creek," still called the Creek. The remaining fourth, comprising twelve acres, was in what is now the compact part of the city; extending from Congress street to the South Mill Pond in one direction, and from Pleasant street to Chestnut street in another. The Episcopal chapel and parsonage described in the Pleasant street Walk already stood on this land, and to the wardens of this church and their successors forever the glebe was entrusted. The first house built on the land after the grant was that of Thomas Phipps, the first Portsmouth school master, built near the North Church. A jail was also built in that neighborhood. No other use was made of " the minister's field " until 1705, when at a town meeting it was ordered to be laid out in house-lots "for peopling the town." This was done, and leases were given for 999 years, at a merely nominal rent. The action had the desired effect, of settling that part of the town which, lying* back from the river, was considered less desirable than the land upon its banks. Up to the date of the Revolution the small rents were regularly collected, since which time no attempt of the kind has been made. At the time of the division of the town into North and South Parishes, their respective rights to the Glebe land were vehemently disputed; though history would apparently adjudge the possession of it to the Episcopal Church. No doubt the question will again be brought forward when the leases expire, but this will not be until the year 2730.

The thirty-eight acres of glebe land which lay beyond the Creek, were left for pasturage until 1790, when Islington road, from the Creek to the Plains, was opened directly through this land. The North Parish, in whose possession the glebe had finally remained, wishing to raise funds to build a parsonage, divided this portion also into lots, and sold leases for 999 years. The parsonage then built was that on Pleasant street.

Stone Church. (Unitarian.)

Built in 1824, by the South Parish, who at that time quitted the old South Church. Their pastor was then Dr. Nathan Parker, who died in 1833, being succeeded by Rev. A. P. Peabody. After a ministry of 27 years, Dr. Peabody left for Cambridge, and in

1862 the present pastor, Rev. James DeNormandie, was ordained.

The site* of this church was the spot where the great fire of 1813 began, on the premises of Mrs. Woodward.

Spence House.

The residence in the last century of Robert Trail, comptroller of the Port of Portsmouth until the Revolution. Mr. Trail was a native of the Orkney Islands, but in what year he came to this country or whether he built this house, is not known. His wife was a sister of Gen. Whipple. *(See Ladd House.)* In 1766 he obtained a patent from government for the exclusive right to brew strong beer in the province, and as the house behind this one, at the corner of Court and Fleet streets, is known by tradition as the first Portsmouth brewery, there is little doubt that Mr. Trail carried on that business there. His daughter married Græme Spence, a Scotchman, and the Spence family resided here for many years. One of the daughters married Dr. Lowell of Cambridge and became the mother of James Russell Lowell, the poet.

Brackett House.

The residence, during the Revolution and later, of Dr. Joshua Brackett, an esteemed physician of the time. He married a sister of Gen. Whipple. His house was formerly much larger than at present.

and the grounds extended back as far as Congress street.

Davenport House.

Built about 1758 by Mrs. Charles Treadwell, *(see National Hotel,)* and given to her son Nathaniel, who resided here. It was afterwards kept for many years as a boarding house by John Davenport, whose name it has retained.

Col. Whipple's House.

The residence of Col. Joseph Whipple, a brother of Gen. William Whipple, and Collector of Customs for the port of Portsmouth. After his death his widow continued to live here; and in 1782, when the Marquis de Chastelleux was in Portsmouth, he speaks in his letter of visiting this lady. He describes her as a lady of understanding and gaiety, and the house itself as being handsome and well furnished.

Rockingham House.

Formerly the residence of Hon. Woodbury Langdon, a brother of Gov. Langdon, born in 1739. He was a successful merchant and a firm patriot, holding many important public offices, among them that of Judge of the Supreme Court.

In 1781 the first great fire in Portsmouth broke out in a barn standing on the site of the present Temple, consuming among other buildings the Jail and Mr. Langdon's house. In 1785 he rebuilt it on the same spot. Mr. Langdon died in 1805. In 1830 the house was purchased by a company of gentlemen who altered it into a public house; and in 1870 it was enlarged and remodelled by Hon. Frank Jones into the present first class hotel.

Baptist Church.

Erected in 1828, when the society was organized under Baron Stowe. (*See Unitarian Chapel.*) The site where it stands was formerly occupied by a small house where lived Shepherd Ham, so called; an eccentric old man who had built on this ledge of rocks. He was a Tory at the time of the Revolution and had taken refuge in Portsmouth from some of the patriots whom he had affronted. He lived in hermit fashion, keeping a herd of half wild ponies and horses, whence his name of Shepherd was derived. His stables extended across the street, and were pulled down when Mason street was opened in 1800.

Windmill Hill.

About 1700 John Pray built a windmill on the highest part of this rise of land, which remained for nearly fifty years. The place was then called Windmill hill, but after Mr. Mason built his house it received the name of Mason's Hill.

Mason House.

Built by Hon. Jeremiah Mason in 1808. Mr. Mason, an eminent lawyer and politician, came to Portsmouth in 1797, when he was twenty-three years old.

In 1813 he was chosen U. S. Senator from New Hampshire. He was remarkable both for his legal abilities and his great personal stature. In 1832 he removed to Boston, where he died in 1848. When this house was built it was on the extreme outskirts of the town ; the grounds were beautiful and extensive. After Mason's death it became the residence of the late Daniel H. Treadwell, father of the present occupant.

Catholic Church.

Before 1853 there was no Catholic place of worship in the city. In that year a wooden church was built on this commanding situation, which was destroyed by fire in 1871. In 1873 the present handsome brick edifice was built.

Portsmouth Pier, and the Fire of 1813.

Before the fire of 1813, Buck street was the chief business mart of Portsmouth, and its most fashionable resort. In this street the first sidewalk was laid. The Pier at its foot was then a scene of great activity, the commerce of the town far exceeding that of the present day. In 1800 no less than 28 ships, 49 brigs and 10 schooners, belonging to Portsmouth, were engaged in foreign commerce ; and in the same year 17 vessels were built here.

The Pier was built in 1796 by the Portsmouth Pier Company, a row of warehouses being erected on each side, surpassing anything of the kind which

then existed in Boston. At the head of the Pier, on
the corner of Water street, stood the first brick house
which was built in Portsmouth, erected by Henry
Sherburne 2d. (*See Sherburne House.*) Mr. Sherburne, who was born in 1674, married Dorothy, sister
of the first Gov. Wentworth, and lived here in a
style of great magnificence. The house remained
in the family until the formation of the Pier Company, who purchased it, and converted it into the New
Hampshire Hotel, where the shipmasters usually
boarded.

Dec. 22, 1813, a fire broke out on the spot where
the Stone Church now stands, which swept over fifteen acres of the central part of the town, entirely de-
stroying this street and Pier. 272 buildings were
burnt, and 130 families made homeless. The business of Portsmouth received a check from this disaster
from which it never recovered.

Episcopal Chapel.

The house which stood on the site of this Chapel,
before the fire of 1813, was formerly the residence of
Rev. John Emerson, pastor of the South Parish,
who died in 1732. That same year Jacob Sheafe
(*See Sheafe house, New Castle,*) removed from New
Castle to Portsmouth, and purchased this house for his
dwelling. A number of years afterward he built a
large mansion on the opposite side of the street
where the house of the late J. M. Tredick now

stands, and removed thither. Mr. Sheafe was a prosperous merchant and a large landowner. He was commissary of the N. H. forces at the capture of Louisburg, and from 1767 to '74 was representative of this town at the General Assembly. He died in 1791, leaving, it is said, to each of his ten children, a house in town and a farm in the vicinity. His son, James, inherited the family mansion. Most of the houses owned by him were destroyed in different conflagrations.

The Episcopal chapel was built in 1832. It contains the first organ ever used in New England, probably the first in America. It was imported in 1713 by Thomas Brattle, for the use of Queen's (now King's) Chapel, Boston. So great was the prejudice against musical instruments, however, that it remained in the vestibule unopened, for several months. It was used in the Chapel until 1756, when it was sold to St. Paul's church, Newburyport, and remained in use there for 80 years. In 1836 it was purchased for this chapel by Dr. Burroughs and put in a new case, but the original pipes and windchest remain. Some of its notes are still of remarkable sweetness.

Brick School House.

This school house is on the site of the old building, which, in 1735 was ceded to the town by Ebenezer Wentworth, in exchange for a lot of land on Daniel street. The only school house previously in use, was the one below the South Mill bridge, to which this was similar in structure, being a large one-story wooden building.

In 1748 Major Samuel Hale opened a school here, which he taught for over 30 years, and, himself a patriot, educated most of our Revolutionary heroes. His title was derived from a company which he commanded at the siege of Louisburg. "His fame," says Alden, "in the regions of the Piscataqua, was equal to that of his contemporary, Master Lowell, in Boston." In 1787 the father of Salmon P. Chase taught here. In 1790 the original building gave place to a handsome brick structure. Other teachers succeeded, of no less note than those we have mentioned. Deacon Amos Tappan and Master Eleazer Taft, among others, kept the High School in one part of the house, while Master Bowles was one of the teachers of a lower school. A room was also reserved in this building for the town clerk and selectmen.

The school house was but partially destroyed by the fire, and was rebuilt in the following year. The building is now used as a school house and Ward room. The Rambles contain many interesting anecdotes of the old school house, and School house hill.

Methodist Church.

Built in 1827. The Methodist society was not organized until 1808, though Jesse Lee preached in Portsmouth as early as 1790. Their first place of worship was the building on Vaughan street, afterwards known as the Cameneum.

Seaman's Home.

In 1832 a society was formed, called the Ladies' Seaman's Friend Society, which in 1835 established a Seaman's Home, which was maintained until 1853. As the number of sailors requiring board in the city had at that time greatly decreased, the Home was discontinued, but not the society; which, however, did not resume active operations until 1875. In that year the present Seaman's Home was opened, which includes a Coffee Room and Free Reading Room.

Court House.

Built in 1836, when the old Court or State house on Market Square was taken down. Its place was previously occupied by an Almshouse. (*See Almshouses.*)

House of Daniel H. Peirce.

Built by John Peirce in 1799. At that time none of the neighbouring houses were standing, and this one was considered to be quite on the outskirts of the town.

Joshua Peirce, (*see Peirce Farm,*) the first of the name in Portsmouth, came here about 1700, and kept a store in his house on the corner of High and Congress streets, where Butler & Laighton's store now stands, which still belongs to his descendants. He was member of the King's Council, and held many important offices, in which his son Daniel— father of John—succeeded him. The family resided in the old house until the erection of this one.

No, 2 Court Street.

All that we know of this house is that it originally stood next south of the North Church, and that in it the "Oracle of the Day," the predecessor of the Portsmouth Journal, was printed by Charles Pierce. The first number was issued in 1793.

Unitarian Chapel.

Built in 1857. The old meeting house which stood on this site, and which was previously used by the South Parish as a chapel, was the Parson Walton meeting house, so called. It was built in 1761 by seceders from Dr. Langdon's and other churches, who called themselves Independent Congregationalists. Rev. Samuel Drown was their first minister. Rev. Joseph Walton was settled over them in 1789, and officiated until a short time before his death in 1822. He was greatly beloved and esteemed. In 1828 the building was purchased by the South Parish as a Sunday school room and chapel, the former occupants having built the Church on Middle street, and organized themselves under Baron Stowe, as the Calvin Baptist Society.

Stavers Hotel,

Built by John Stavers in 1770, as a tavern, with the sign of the Earl of Halifax. It was the principal hotel in the town. For a time it was the chief rendezvous of the tory party, and in 1777 was attacked by a mob and much injured. When fitted up again the sign was changed to William Pitt, and it was called the Pitt Hotel, giving its name to the street. Mr. Stavers became friendly to the cause of the nation, and often entertained the officers of the Revolution at his house. In 1782 Lafayette stayed here, and in 1789 it was here that Washington took leave of the State authorities after his visit.

The Halifax hotel referred to in Longfellow's poem of "Lady Wentworth," is not this one, but one previously kept by Mr. Stavers on Queen street, now State street. While there, in 1761, he commenced running a weekly stage coach to Boston, which is supposed to have been the first one run in America. It was called the "Flying Stage Coach," and carried but three passengers. It left Portsmouth Monday morning. stopped that night at Ipswich, and left Boston on its return Thursday morning. When Mr. Stavers occupied the hotel on Pitt street, the coach was kept in the large stable still standing adjacent to the house.

Underwood House.

This is one of our oldest houses. It was built about 1700 by John Underwood, who married a sister of Margery Bray, (*see Bray house*,) and removed hither from Kittery. The house is still in possession of some of his descendants. A tradition lingers in the family of undiscovered treasures beneath an old hearthstone in one of the ancient rooms.

Atkinson House.

This fine old mansion, which resembled in appearance the Pepperrell house in Kittery, was built about 1734 by Theodore Atkinson 2d, Secretary of the Province of N. H., and one of the most eminent men of his time.

When Col. Mason sold his title to the N. H. grant in 1746, (*see Mason House,*) Atkinson purchased one-fifth of it. He was very wealthy, and his house was said to contain more silver ware than any other in the State. It was handsomely fitted up, and the grounds embraced nearly all the neighborhood.

Atkinson was an excellent man, and devoted to religion. At his death he left a legacy of about $1000 to the St. John's Church, the income to be dispensed in bread to the poor, which is still done. He died in 1779, and his son having died before him, the property, including the mansion, passed into the hands of a relative, who took his name.

His son, Theodore Atkinson, jr. who had succeeded his father as Secretary, died on the 28th of October, 1769, and was buried in great state; and two weeks after, (Nov. 11,) his widow was married to Gov. John Wentworth, her cousin, to whom she had been attached in early life.

Walk Fourth.

Market Square, Congress and Islington Streets.

Market Square, or the Parade, as it used to be called, will now be our starting point for another walk. Standing on the steps of the Athenæum,* we will look around the Square itself. Directly in front you see the North Church,* and to the left, beside blocks of stores, two noticeable brick edifices, the first of which is devoted to banks and offices, while the other contains the city rooms. This was, until lately, Jefferson Market* and Jefferson Hall.* The old State House,* or Court House, stood nearly in the centre of the Square,* where now are usually seen hay carts or wood carts, and dealers in country produce of all kinds.

Turning to the right to walk up Congress street, you will see at one glance several sites of historical interest; the building at the corner* of narrow Church street, the Rogers block,* the National Hotel* and the block* next to it; while on the right are Congress block,* and the site of the old Bell Tavern* adjoining. Crossing Fleet street, you have Franklin Hall* on the right, and opposite, the gambrel roofed building where is located Plumer's bakeshop,* and the vacant Melcher* site. Chestnut street, on the left, will lead to the Temple,* and Vaughan street on the right is a direct route to the various railroad depots. At its further corner are the Young People's Union Rooms,* and opposite, the Kearsarge House,* Col. Peirce's house,* Miss Leavitt's,* and Misses Cutter's,* all places of historical interest. At the southern corner of Middle street is the Academy,* the first building in Islington street, as the street changes its name at this point. No. 2 is the Buckminster house,* and the two old houses that you soon come to, Nos. 6 and 7, are called the Kennard house* and the Remick house.* As you go on, the little streets that you pass on the right lead to the Steam Factory,* and on one of them stands the pretty little Freewill Baptist Church.

The houses on the left are not very old. The Haven house, next to the Academy, was built in 1800 by John Haven, oldest son of Dr. Sam. Haven, and the Parker house, No. 5, in 1790. No. 21, the residence of Charles W. Brewster, the author of the "Rambles about Portsmouth," was built in 1817, and A. R. H. Fernald's on the corner of Summer street in 1797. If you were to turn off into Summer street you would have a pleasant stroll through the shaded labyrinth of streets that lie between Islington and Middle streets; but we will go straight on, past the Hussey house,* No. 16, standing on what was once Rock Pasture, the Jail*—the old and the new buildings—the Haliburton house,* No. 25, and No. 40, the residence of our honored ex-Governor Goodwin. At the head of Brewster street are two large stone posts, one marked 1795; but they are of recent erection.

On Langdon street stands the Partingtonian mansion,* known by name to every visitor. But the short streets on the right usually lead only to obscure localities and to the once lovely North Mill Pond. The Fitzgerald house,* at the corner of Union street, is the only one which can be mentioned, although we pass other old buildings, until you arrive at the Creek.

Turning to the right and crossing the bridge, you pass the Breweries, the old Ham house* and the house above it, which has an ancient look, but was built within the present century. Creek street, which curves to the left as you go on, leads by the fine house and grounds of the late Hon. Levi Woodbury* and near the Almshouse.* If you follow it out of the city you will reach Hon. Frank Jones' farm,* and Newington. If you turn to the right down Woodbury or Myrtle streets, you will go round the North Pond to Christian Shore. Boyd's road, which opens close beside the Woodbury mansion, leads to pleasant farms and to Fountain Head.*

If, when you reach the Creek, you go on up Islington Road instead of crossing the bridge, you will pass Frenchman's Lane* and the Powder house, and reach the Plains.

Athenæum.

In 1817 a society was incorporated with the title of "Proprietors of the Portsmouth Athenæum," which founded the Institution so called. It is not a public library, as only the shareholders can use the books. It is owned in 100 shares, and has a library of over 11,000 volumes, besides periodicals and newspapers. The building in which it is kept was erected for the use of the Fire and Marine Insurance Company, incorporated in 1803. From the roof of the Athenæum a fine view of the city and neighborhood can be obtained.

North Church (Trinitarian).

In the earliest Portsmouth records the spot where the North Church now stands was called the Fort, or the Great Fort, but the reason for this is not apparent. The first church here was built in 1712. Previous to this time the only place of worship in town, (after the disappearance of the Chapel on Pleasant street,) was the one below the mill dam, the minister being supported from the town taxes. As the number of inhabitants increased, this meeting house was found to be small, and too far from the centre of the town, and in 1711 it was voted in town meeting to build a new one on this spot, to take the place of the old one. But a large minority deemed this locality too far north, preferring a place in Pleasant street, (*see Joseph Haven's house,*) and a quarrel began which lasted for a generation. When the house was built here, a separation took place; the minister, Rev. Nathaniel Rogers, going with a part of the parish to the new building, taking with them the church records and plate; while the remainder, led by Capt. John Pickering, continued to worship at the old meeting house, and called Rev. John Emerson, of New Castle, to be their pastor. The important question, which parish should have the glebe land and the town taxes for the support of their minister, was referred to an ecclesiastical council from Massachusetts, who decided in favor of the South Parish; then to a general Council of the Province of New Hampshire, who adjudged the glebe land to the North Parish, but declared both North and South to be town parishes, and equally entitled to the town taxes. But this decision satisfied no one; and so much injustice was shown in apportioning the taxes that in 1716 it was agreed that each parish should pay its own minister, —and here the matter rested.

In 1745 the town clock was put up. The old church stood until 1854, when it was taken down and the present one was built.

Jefferson Market and Hall.

The site of this building was formerly occupied by

an old house belonging to James Grouard, who kept a hat store in front, and let a large chamber over it for singing schools and other public uses. Here the first town school for girls was kept in 1784-5, after which no school of the kind was maintained until 1815.

In 1800 the town bought this lot, and built a market with a town hall over it, which the next year received the name of Jefferson, in honor of the newly elected President. In the fire of 1802 all but the brick walls was consumed; in 1804 it was rebuilt. In 1818 the Hall was first used, instead of the old State house, for election purposes, and town meetings were held here until the adoption of a city charter in 1849. In 1864 the Hall was cut up and altered into City Rooms; in 1873 the outside of the building was remodelled, and in 1875 the market was abolished.

Old State House.

Built in 1758 upon a ledge of rocks, occupying the centre of our present Square. In this building the courts and all public meetings were held; the Masons had one room in it, and the Fire Companies another. In the time of the Revolution the patriots held enthusiastic meetings here, and from its steps —facing on King street—the Declaration of Independence was read to an excited multitude. When the reading was finished, Thomas Manning proposed that the name of King street should be at once changed to Congress street, which was carried by acclamation.

In 1788, when New Hampshire adopted the Federal Constitution, being the ninth State to do so, the event was celebrated with great rejoicings. On that occasion, "the State House was beautifully illuminated with nine lights in each window, while a large company of ladies and gentlemen, on the Parade, were entertained with music from the balcony." In 1789 Washington was formally received by the citizens, on the balcony over the eastern door.

The old State House was removed in 1837, when the Court House on Court street was built. Part of it is still standing, altered into a dwelling house— No. 47 Court street.

Market Square.

The open space so called did not exist in its present proportions till the State House was taken down. When the State House was built, in 1758, the site of the present Rockingham Bank was occupied by the house of John Fisher, and the residence of Nathaniel Adams stood on the corner of State and Pleasant streets, no houses being between. A row of large elms bordered the street, under which the militia used to drill, which originated the name of the Parade, afterward extended to the whole square. These elms were destroyed in the fire of 1813.

Directly in front of the Rockingham Bank stood a brick watch house, which was taken down at the time of Washington's visit in 1789, at which time the ledge of rocks across the street was also removed.

House at the corner of Church Street.

The house of Hunking Wentworth stood here at the time of the Revolution. He was the uncle of Gov. John Wentworth, and, unlike his nephew, a zealous patriot. In his home the Committee of Public Safety held their meetings.

Rogers House.

On this spot was built the house of Thomas Phipps, first public schoolmaster in Portsmouth. (*See Glebe land*.)

In 1704 the house of Rev. Nathaniel Rogers, on Pleasant street, (probably the old Episcopal parsonage,) was burnt down, one of his children and two other members of his family perishing in the flames. The next year, with the assistance of the parish, he built this house; which is said to have been the first one in town in which square panes of glass were used instead of the diamond shaped.

Mr. Rogers was a son of President Rogers of Harvard College, and a most excellent man. He was pastor of the parish from 1697 to his death in 1723. He was buried at the Point of Graves, but his monument, if remaining, is illegible. The house remained in the family until within a few years; but has since then been entirely remodelled.

Block adjoining National Hotel.

This block, now occupied by W. Freeman and others, stands on the site of the house which was built in 1728 by Charles Treadwell. Mr. Treadwell came from Ipswich in 1724. His wife was a woman of remarkable energy, intelligence and piety, who, with her husband carried on for many years an extensive business in provisions and furnishing goods, and acquired a large fortune. Their store was in their dwelling house on this spot, and was the chief market in Portsmouth for country produce, etc. They built some of the best houses in Portsmouth. Mrs. Treadwell's portrait, undoubtedly by Copley, is preserved by one of her descendants.

National Hotel.

Built by Mr. Treadwell, about 1745, for his only daughter Hannah, who afterwards married Dr. Ammi R. Cutter.

Dr. Cutter was born in Maine, in 1735, and came to Portsmouth to study medicine with Dr. Clement Jackson. After completing his studies, he became surgeon of a New Hampshire Regiment, and was with them through the French and Indian war. After the capture of Louisburg in 1758 he returned and commenced practice here. But during the Revolution he again joined the army, being in charge of the medical department in the northern army until the peace. He was an eminent and highly respected physician. During the yellow fever in 1798 he was devoted to the sufferers, exposing himself to the danger fearlessly. His son, Dr. William Cutter, and Dr. Brackett were equally faithful, the former taking the disease, to which he nearly fell a victim. It was Dr. William Cutter who built the brick mansion on this street, now occupied by A. W. Haven. He died in 1817, and his father in 1820.

In 1840 this house was remodelled into the Mansion House, afterward called City Hotel, and now kept as the National Hotel.

Congress Block.

The first knowledge that we have of this spot is, that in 1738, a house was burnt down here, which had been occupied by Robert Macklin, an old baker, who lived to the age of 115 years. Soon after the fire, a part of the old meeting house at the South Mill bridge was removed hither and converted into a dwelling house, by a merchant named John Newmarch. After his death the house was occupied by one of his daughters, who had married Richard Billings, clerk at one time to John Hancock, and a citizen of some distinction. His store, for groceries and pewter ware, was in one corner of his dwelling. The Billings house was taken down in 1846 to make room for Congress block. Some of the original windows of the old meeting house remained until the demolition of the house; they consisted of diamond-shaped panes about four inches square.

In 1864 Congress block was burnt down, but was soon rebuilt, the upper stories being elegantly fitted up for Masonic purposes.

Bell Tavern.

Built in 1743 by Paul March, a rich merchant, who occupied it, but whether as a tavern or not we do not know. He married a daughter of John Newmarch, who lived next door. Previous to the Revolution the house was kept as a tavern by John Greenleaf, with the sign of a Bluebell hanging from a post in front. This tavern was the headquarters of the patriotic party, as the Halifax hotel was of the tories. It was here that the Marquis of Chastelleux boarded in 1782, when the French fleet, of which he was commander, was in the harbor. The house was kept as a tavern until 1852, and was the scene of many interesting incidents. The Probate Court met here for many years. It was burnt in 1867.

Franklin House.

This building was originally two dwelling houses, built by Langley Boardman at the beginning of the present century, and soon after converted into a tavern, known as the Stage House. In 1819 the part on the corner of Fleet street, (then Mason street,) was built, containing a hall for assemblies, called Franklin Hall, and one over it for the Masons. The whole house was then named Franklin House. The old hall was afterwards cut up into rooms, but has been handsomely restored by the present owner, Alfred Stavers.

After the days of Stavers' Flying Coach (*see Stavers Hotel*,) and before the era of railroads, this tavern was the headquarters of two Stage Companies, whose drivers and coaches had a reputation for carefulness, comfort and speed second to none in the country. One, which ran coaches between Boston and Portsmouth, had its stable on Washington street, while the stable of the Portland Stage Company was on Hanover street. In this tavern was the booking office, not only for both these routes, but for all the smaller country stages, and here Mendum, Annable, Robinson, Barnabee, and other "Knights of the Whip," who ruled the road in a style that Dickens would have admired, were wont to hold their court.

Plumer's Bakeshop.

Built about 1784, by Nathaniel Dean, who in that year came here from Exeter. He occupied the house for about 40 years. Previously, there stood on this site the house of Dr. Moses, of eccentric memory. His widow, "Marm Moses," kept a school here at the time of the Revolution.

Melcher House.

The Melcher house, which was burnt on this spot in 1873, was originally a fine gambrel roof building, owned by the Boyd family. Col. Boyd lived here before he bought the Livius estate (*see Raynes house,*) in 1768. From 1780 to 1790 it was occupied by Robert Gerrish, who printed the N. H. Mercury here. John Melcher who afterwards resided here, was an apprentice of Robert Fowle, and succeeded him as publisher of the N. H. Gazette.

Temple.

The site of the so-called Temple was formerly occupied by the first Portsmouth Almshouse, built in 1716 and used until 1755. Chestnut street was then named Prison Lane, and Warren street, Fetter Lane, from the Jail which stood at the corner of the two.

The present edifice was built in 1803 as a Free Will Baptist Church, and was used for religious purposes until 1844, when it was taken by the Washingtonian Temperance Society, (then at the height of their activity,) and remodelled for a lecture room. As such it has ever since been used, having been repeatedly altered and adorned. It has always been the favorite lyceum and exhibition hall of Portsmouth.

Young People's Union Rooms.

Established in 1871. They are intended as a pleasant and safe evening resort for young people of both sexes. They consist of an amusement room furnished with games of all sorts, and a reading room, supplied with periodicals and a large library.

Kearsarge House.

Built by Col. Peirce as dwelling houses, but converted into a hotel soon after. The place where it stands was occupied by a house built about 1735 by Jacob Treadwell, a brother of Charles. He was a tanner, and his tan yard was in Bridge street. His son Nathaniel afterwards occupied the house; and from him have descended most of the Portsmouth families named Treadwell.

Col, Pierce's House.

Built about 1785 by William Sheafe, son of Jacob. Here he died in 1839, aged 81. The house then passed into the possession of the late Col. Peirce, a son of John Peirce. *(See Peirce House, Court street.)*

Miss Leavitt's House.

The first mention of this house that we find is that Hon. Wyseman Clagett removed hither from the Hart house, Daniel street, (q. v.) after the fire of 1761, and lived here several years. He married Lettice Mitchell, *(see Mitchell house,)* and proved himself as harsh a master at home as he was severe and unscrupulous in his public capacity. He was King's Attorney, appointed 1758, and Justice of the Peace. To be "Clagetted" was a common term for being persecuted. Nevertheless he was a friend to his country, and a member of the Committee of Safety during the Revolution. He afterwards removed to Litchfield, where he died in 1784.

Misses Cutter's House.

Built about 1750 by Charles Treadwell, for his son Jacob. The house afterwards became the property ot Dr. Ammi R. Cutter, and was given by him to his daughter, who married Col. Storer and was long known among our citizens as Madam Storer. This beautifully finished mansion, containing many curious memorials, is still in possession of the family.

Academy.

Built about 1800 by a society incorporated for the purpose, and intended for private schools. It was used as such until 1868, when it was let to the city for public schools. It contains a grammar school for bŏys, one for girls, and an intermediate school for girls.

Buckminster House.

This handsome building was erected in 1720 by Daniel Warner, father of Jonathan, (*see Warner house*,) and of Nathaniel, who was engaged to Miss Lettice Mitchell, and for whom this house was designed. It afterwards passed through various hands, and in 1792 was purchased by Col. Eliphalet Ladd, who resided here until his death in 1806. In 1810 Dr. Buckminster married Col. Ladd's widow, and left the Parsonage house on Pleasant street, to reside in this mansion. Since then it has usually been called by his name, though his death occurred in 1812.

Kennard House.

Built about 1700 and kept formerly as the Eagle tavern, though very little can be ascertained about it. The only incident recorded is that at the time of a very deep snow, in the latter part of April, 1717, a child was born in this house, and the doctor and nurse entered at the chamber window. This snow is said to have been eight feet on a level, and for years was spoken of as the "great snow."

Remick House.

Built in 1696, by Daniel Remark (or Remick) and others. It was long known as the Jenny Stewart house, from one of its former owners. The house being built upon a ledge of rocks, it was necessary to dig the well, (at that time essential to every house,) on the opposite side of the road. This well has been in use until within a few years.

When the house was repaired in 1851, a jug was found imbedded in the masonry, containing wine; and under the hearthstone several bushels of salt were discovered, which had been placed there more than 150 years before.

Steam Factory. (Kearsarge Mills.)

The site of this factory was formerly the residence of Nathaniel Adams, the author of the Annals of Portsmouth; the house standing where the factory now stands, while the garden and grounds extended from Rock to Parker streets, and from the pond to Islington street. This fine estate was the property, in the last century, of William Parker, an English gentleman, who married a daughter of the Earl of Derby, against her father's wishes, and came with her to this country in 1703. He purchased this spot for his residence, and took up the trade of a tanner, his tanyard being situated on what has ever since been called Tanner street. One of his sons, William, became an eminent lawyer and Judge of the Superior Court, from which office he was removed at the time of the Revolution.   John, another son, was the father of Noah Parker, the first Universalist minister in Portsmouth, whose early life was passed in this house. His daughter Elizabeth married Capt. Nathaniel Adams, the father of the Annalist.

The spot was purchased in 1845 by a company formed for the purpose, and the Portsmouth Steam Factory was erected.   Two years after it was built the roof blew off in a high gale, but fortunately no one was injured.   At first the factory was used for the manufacture of lawns; but in 1863 the machinery was changed, and the manufacture of spool cotton was introduced.   In 1865 the price of cotton fell one-half, while the company had a large quantity on hand, and from this and other causes they failed. The mill was then sold, and the purchasers gave it the name of Kearsarge Mills, and put in looms for weaving sheeting, shirting and jeans.   For some years only the jeans have been manufactured here. About 300 hands are employed, and 2500 bales of cotton used per year.

Hussey House.

The site of this house was formerly occupied by a huge rock, which gave its name to Rock Pasture. The house was built in 1812 by Joshua Haven, a son of Dr. Samuel Haven; the cellar being excavated from the solid rock.

Rock Pasture.

The land lying beyond the factory, between Islington Road and the pond, was formerly so designated. It was a favorite resort for boys; and an old cellar, over which now stands No. 10 Langdon street, was a great attraction. The tradition was that the whole pasture had been purchased by a rich Englishman, named Myrick, who intended to lay out a handsome park on the borders of the then beautiful creek. The cellar had been dug for his proposed house, but, wishing to visit England on business, he left for that country, first concealing his gold in the cellar or its vicinity. He was probably lost at sea, for nothing more was heard of him, nor was anything ever heard of his treasure, unless it was found by the foreman of the neighboring ropewalk, who became suddenly rich in an unaccountable manner. *(See Boyd estate.)*

Jail.

The first jail in Portsmouth was built in 1699 on Congress street, near the corner of Fleet street, on the glebe land, but the exact spot is not known. It was a strong log house, 30 by 14 ft. square. In 1759 another was built on the southern corner of Warren and Chestnut streets, constructed of oak timber hewn square and covered with iron bars, and lined with plank. This stronghold was burnt in the fire of 1781, when Woodbury Langdon's house was destroyed. The flames from the burning jail were so intensely hot that the firemen could only work a few minutes

at a time, while engaged in saving Col. Whipple's
house. (*See Davenport house.*)   In 1782 the present
wooden jail was built, the stone jail adjoining being
erected fifty years later.   At first the latter was of
one story only, but as the cells were found to be un-
healthy, another story was added, and the lower cells
were disused.

Halliburton House.

Nothing is known of the origin of this ancient
looking house.   It was moved to this spot from the
South End, and remodelled to its present proportions,
according to immemorial Portsmouth usage, which
rarely allows a house to be pulled down.   It was the
residence of the late Andrew Halliburton.   Mr. Halliburton was born in Nova Scotia, in the year 1771,
and was a cousin of Judge Haliburton, author of "Sam
Slick."   He came to Portsmouth in 1791, was Dep-
uty Collector, and afterward Cashier of the Portsmouth Bank for thirty years.   He died in 1846.   His
upright character and literary talents made him a
man of much social eminence.

Partingtonian Mansion.

At the foot of Langdon street, on the left hand,
stands a small one-story house, the "little house by
the river," where lived the parents of Benjamin P.
Shillaber.   Here too, resided his aunt, the prototype
of the immortal Mrs. Ruth Partington.

Fitzgerald House.

Built in 1724 by a Mr. Mead; the timber for the
house being cut from the forest behind it.   Mr.

Mead's daughter married Richard Fitzgerald, and occupied the house. Their son Richard was born here in 1771, and here he lived until his death in 1858, aged 87. His wife, aged 78, died the same day. In his garden grew a rose bush which bore roses for over eighty years. The house has been somewhat altered.

Creek and North Pond.

That the name of Creek was always given to this bay is proved from the Glebe land grant, dated 1640, in which it is called Strawberry Bank Creek. In 1659 the selectmen granted leave to John Cutt to build a sawmill and cornmill "on the creek leading up to the fresh marsh," with the condition that he was to grind corn for the town whenever required. The grist mill was built where the brook from beyond the brewery formerly emptied, and there the remains of the old dam can yet be seen. The brook now falls into the pond further to the west.

Cutt's mill stood until after the building of Livius' mills. (See *North Mill.*) The sawmill stood on the other side of the present Creek bridge; it remained until all the forest in the neighborhood, pine and oak, was cut away, when it was taken down. Quite a little village collected here, which was called Islington, giving its name to the road and creek. Before the building of the Livius mills, there was a direct connexion of this part of the town with the harbor, and the pond was a fine sheet of water on which ships sailed, and where vessels were built. There were

two ropewalks in the vicinity near the present Eastern Depot, and the banks of the pond were more
thickly settled than the centre of the town.   Even in
later years, until the railroad to Boston and, since
then, the breweries were built, the North pond was a
beautiful place, and had many pleasant residences
upon its banks.

Among the noted dwellers on its shores was James
Mifflin, called the Commodore.   He was an English
soldier who had fought at the battle of Bunker Hill,
and was taken prisoner by our troops.   Not being
exchanged, he was after a while set free, and came
to live here, establishing himself close to the edge of
the pond.   He was called Commodore Mifflin from
the fleet of boats he gathered under his supervision,
and was an eminent character among the boys of
the town.

In 1830 a hosiery factory was established at the
Creek, but it failed of success, and having been shut
up for years was partially burned, and at last was tak-
en down in 1858 to make room for the large brewery
which now stands here.

Ham House.

This is one of the oldest houses in town.   The
precise date of its erection is not known; but it was
formerly a two-story building, and when it was cut
down to its present dimensions, it was found to be
filled in between the beams and rafters, with stones

and stubble, to make it arrow proof, leaving little doubt that it was built as a garrison house.

The cellar kitchen is provided with wide doors to receive the hogsheads of molasses and rum that were stored there, when its owner, one of Mr. Ham's ancestors, carried on a thriving West India trade. The schooners could then come up the Creek, and land their valuable cargoes at his very door.

Woodbury Mansion.

Built in 1809 by Capt. Samuel Ham, who after the house was finished, gave a large party to celebrate the event. When the guests had departed, he, for some unknown reason, went into one of the upper chambers and hung himself.

When Hon. Levi Woodbury came to Portsmouth in 1819 he purchased this elegant house and grounds. He was born in Francestown in 1789; in 1823 he was chosen Governor of the State. He afterwards became U. S. Senator, Secretary of the Treasury under Jackson, and in 1841 was appointed Judge of the Supreme Court in place of Judge Story. He was always a leading Democrat, and was thought to be a probable candidate for the Presidency at the time of his death in 1851. The house is still in possession of the family, although they make it only occasional summer visits.

Almshouse.

The first almshouse in Portsmouth was built in 1716, on the site of the Temple on Chestnut street. It was the first building of the kind ever erected in this country, or indeed in any country, as it was not until 1723 that similar workhouses were built in England. In 1755 it was replaced by one on the site of the present Court House, the old almshouse being sold. The first keeper of the new house was Clement March, grandfather of the late N. B. March, who served in that capacity from 1755 to 1790. The building was also used as a town house, and for selectmen's meetings. In 1770 a house of correction was built in the workhouse yard.

In 1833 a farm of 165 acres was purchased of the heirs of Thomas Sheafe, for a town farm, and the present Almshouse was erected in the following year. In 1869 a County Poor-house was established at Brentwood; and from that time only the city poor have been sent to this place; a great part of the farm is to be sold in consequence.

Hon. Frank Jones' Farm.

This land was originally the property of Hon. George Atkinson, who succeeded to Theodore Atkinson's house and estate. (*See Atkinson house.*) He died in 1790, and the farm passed into possession of the related family of Sparhawks. It is now the property of our present Representative at Washington.

Fountain Head.

In 1797 a company was incorporated by the name of the Portsmouth Aqueduct Company, who purchased the springs at the so-called Oak hill farm, about 2 1-2 miles from Market Square, which now bear the name of Fountain Head. They were formerly known as the Warm Springs, because the water never freezes, coming apparently from a great depth. The water was brought into town in wooden logs, and being of the very best quality, has been of incalculable benefit to the inhabitants. The place itself lies in the midst of marshy woods, rather difficult of access.

Of late years the supply of water being inadequate for the increased demand, in 1866 a spring was added, situated near the Concord Railroad; and in 1875 a still further supply was procured from the Scott farm in Newington, the springs at the latter place being said to be inexhaustible.

Frenchman's Lane.

It was not until 1792 that the direct road from the Creek to the Plains, known as Islington road, was opened. The old road was a very circuitous one, part of which remains as Frenchman's Lane. Before the Eastern Railroad crossed it, it was a delightful spot, much frequented by boys and pedestrians, as was also a shady little retreat in the neighborhood, called McDonough's dell, through which flowed the brook, now polluted and half dried up.

Frenchman's Lane derives its name from a Frenchman named John Dushan, who was robbed and murdered on the night of Oct. 23, 1778. His body was found the next morning lying on a flat stone in this lane. The authors of the crime were never discovered; but it gave a new and fearful interest to the place.

When the Sons of Portsmouth had their first reunion in their native city on July 4th, 1853, it was here that a thousand of them were landed from the cars, and marched home with music and banners.

Walk Fifth.

Middle Street and the West End.

If from Congress street you turn off to the left by the Academy, you enter the long, curving street, known by the unexpressive name of Middle street. It affords a pleasant walk, but not through a histori-cal part of the town. It was opened in 1737, when George Jaffrey sold to the town "a highway three rods wide, leading from the county road from Ports-mouth up to Islington; running southwesterly from the front of Dr. Ross' house." Dr. Ross lived in a house on the site now occupied by 89 Congress street. But though opened so long ago, it was not immedi-ately settled. Until the present century there were scarcely any houses between the Academy and Wi-bird's Hill, now Wibird street; on the left hand the solitary one being the Langdon house, the residence of the late Samuel Lord.* Of the few on the right, not one is now standing; so that we look in vain for old houses here.

Passing the North Parish Chapel and the Langdon house, with its elegant grounds, you cross Haymar-

ket Square.*   Keeping to the left of the Baptist church
you pass among some of the finest modern houses in
the city.   Richards Avenue* opens to the left, leading
to the cemeteries, Sagamore Creek and Rye.   Austin
and Summer streets turn to the right, the handsome
house standing No. 1 on the former street, being the
residence of the late J. P. Lyman.   Both these streets
afford a pleasant, shaded walk on a summer day.

Middle street leads on past the stately Rundlett
mansion out to the suburbs of the city, the right hand
being the older part, while the left is but recently settled.   In the older section few of the houses have any
known history.   No. 23* on Union street, formerly
Anthony, is an exception.   Wibird street, formerly
Wibird's Hill,* bears a historical name. On Miller avenue stands Miss Morgan's Seminary; and the Avenue if pursued, will lead to Lincoln Hill.*   From
this hill, and from the streets running over what was
called Rundlett's Mountain, fine views of the city can
be obtained, and occasionally a glimpse of the White
Mountains.   Middle Road leads out of the city to the
Plains and Greenland.

Residence of the late Samuel Lord.

This house was built some time previous to the
Revolution, but the exact date is not known.   It was
erected by Capt. Purcell, a merchant, one of whose
seven daughters married Major Gardiner, and another Capt. Thomas Manning. After Capt. Purcell's
death, his widow kept a boarding house here, and

John Paul Jones boarded with her during the year
1779, while he was superintending the building of the
ship America. (*See Islands in Harbor*.) The house
afterward passed into the hands of Hon. John Langdon, and from his family it was purchased by the late
Samuel Lord.

Haymarket Square.

In the year 1755 the record stands that "a Haymarket, with convenient scales for weighing, was erected
near Middle Road." At that time it was on the very
outskirts of the town, and as such it was considered for
the next fifty years. The Hayscales stood until within thirty years, giving the name Haymarket Square
to the open space around them.

When the Sons of Portsmouth made their second
visit home, in 1873, this spot was the headquarters of
the New York company. They gave it the name of
Manhattan Square, and would have supplied it with
a flagstaff if the name could have been retained.
But the title was too imposing for so limited a space,
and the old familiar designation was resumed.

Richards Avenue.

Called in old times Cow Lane; afterwards digni-
fied with the name of Joshua street, from Col. Joshua
Wentworth, who lived on the site now occupied by
Henry H. Ladd's house. When the Proprietors' Burying Ground was laid out, in 1830, the street received
the name of Auburn street, and the cemetery was
usually called the Auburn-street Cemetery.

In 1861 and the year following, the beautiful avenue of trees extending the whole length of the street was planted, mainly through the personal exertions of Dr. Robert O. Treadwell and Henry L. Richards: and after the death of the latter upon the field of Gettysburg, the name was changed to Richards Avenue in honor of his memory.

Mrs. Mary Cutts, who died in 1869, left a bequest of $14,000, to be laid out in improvements upon the Avenue, which money has just been expended.

The only house of historical interest in the street is the last one on the left hand, No. 15. This was built in 1751 as a town school house, on School street, and was removed hither and made into a dwelling house when the brick Bartlett school house was erected.

House No. 23 Union Street.

Built after the war of 1812, by John & N. A. Haven, for a negro named John Francis, in gratitude for a service rendered by him during the war. A valuable ship owned by the Messrs. Haven having been captured by the British, Francis succeeded in secreting $15,000 in gold, the proceeds of the sale of the cargo, in a slush tub. He served on board under the new owners until land was reached, when he begged the slush tub with its greasy contents for his perquisite, and restored the money safely to its owners.

Wibird's Hill.

Named from Richard Wibird or one of his sons,

who owned land here. Richard Wibird, in 1727, was the most wealthy man in Portsmouth, paying the highest tax and owning five houses. He is said to have built the first brick house in town. He died in 1732. His son Richard was appointed member of his Majesty's Council in 1739, and in 1756 Judge of Probate. He died in 1765; his brother Thomas died the same year, leaving in his will enough silver to make two large flagons for the North Church, which are still in use.

Lincoln Hill.

This is considered to be the highest part of Portsmouth. Here formerly grew seven lofty pines, which formed a landmark for seamen entering the harbor. The hill was named after them " Seven pine hill;" the land in the vicinity, "Packer's Pasture," being the property of Sheriff Packer. *(See Page* 8.*)* Its present name was given to it by F. W. Miller, whose pleasant residence now adorns it, and to whose public spirit and enterprise, followed up by that of B. F. Webster, it is mainly owing that fine streets and cheerful houses have taken the place of the former rocks and pastures.

Walk Sixth.

Vaughan, High and Deer Streets.

The two principal streets that turn off from Congress street to the right are Vaughan and High streets. Vaughan street, though usually regarded only as a passage to the Eastern Depot, is a very interesting place to antiquarians, containing several memorable buildings. The first house to be noticed is the Pickering house,* on the left, now called the American House, behind which stands a stable, once the Cameneum.* Directly after, you see a stately three-story mansion facing you, having a garden in front, protected by a high fence. This is the Mason House.* It stands on the corner of Hanover street, formerly Cross street, on which you can see, a few steps to the right, the Johnson house,* usually so called. A little farther up Vaughan street you come to the old Assembly house* on the left, now divided into two by Raitt's Court: while nearly opposite stands the handsome Meserve house.* No. 25 was the abode of Rev. Samuel Drown,* next are J. S. Treat's marble works,* and opposite is the old Toppan mansion. Vaughan street

now crosses Deer street, and goes on past Russell
and Green streets, as far as the wharves and the harbor on the North side of the city. Old houses abound,
whose history the visitor would be glad to know;
but as we do not know it, we will go back to Congress street, and turn up High street. This is an
ancient looking, narrow street, less of a thoroughfare
than Vaughan, and retaining still some of the old
flagged sidewalks. The stately square mansion on
the left is the Haven mansion*—and next to it the
residence, for some time, of Daniel Webster.* Farther on you see some very old dwellings—one of the
oldest, with quaint blinds, is known as Rev. Jabez
Fitch's abode :* the history of the others has not been
traced. We now reach Deer street again. Deer
street begins at Market street; at the Northern corner of the two stood, until within a few years, one of
our most interesting relics of the past, the old
Vaughan house :* but having been degraded to a low
boarding house, it was at last pulled down; but
Deer street has plenty of old houses left. The third
from the corner of Market street was once a hotel
with the sign of a Deer, whence the street derived its
name. Next stands a house with the date of its erection, 1705, painted on its chimney, though modern
improvements have deprived it of its other marks of
age. All we know of it is that it was built in that
year by John Newmarch, (see Congress Block,) to
whom also belonged the Deer Hotel. You now see,

across its garden, the Hart house,* which fronts on
Russell street, and then two handsome houses, back
from the road, with fine old trees before them. The
first is the Jenness house,*—of the second we only
know that it was built by Henry Sherburne 2d. *(See
Sherburne House.)*

The next one, the Rice House, was built by Daniel
Hart; and the last on this side of the street was erected by Michael Whidden, the builder of the Assembly
House and others. Of none of these have we the exact dates. The last mentioned belonged to the Underwood family, and this corner was long known as
Underwood's corner. The only house on the other
side of the street whose antecedents we know, is the
Dupray house, No. 15, where lived of old, Deacon
Joseph Cotton, a zealous member of Father Walton's
congregation, *(see Unitarian Chapel,)* and renowned
for his gift in prayer.

Crossing Vaughan street, we come to the Eastern
R. R. Depot,* and then, passing the Brewster House,
built in 1766, and the older Livius House,* we reach
the Concord Depot.*

Pickering House.

Built about 1780 by Edward Hart. At the time it
was built, the tide from the North pond flowed as far
as this spot, (the salt grass was said to be as high
as a man's head,) showing how nearly enclosed by the
sea Portsmouth originally was.

Mr. Hart was, at this time, the only baker in Portsmouth, and the livery stable adjoining the house was built for his bake-house. The hot bread was at first carried round to customers on a horse's back, in panniers, but this was found to be injurious to the horse, and a cart was substituted.

The house afterward passed into the hands of Judge John Pickering, a direct descendant of John Pickering 1st, *(see South Mill,)* and the immediate ancestor of many of our Portsmouth families.

Cameneum.

Built in 1784 for a Universalist church, of which Rev. Noah Parker was the first pastor. It was occupied as such until 1808 when the church on Pleasant street was built. It was then purchased by the Methodists and used until 1827. In 1831 it was fitted up for a theatre, and a few years after was adapted for a lyceum hall. Rev. Dr. Burroughs made an opening address on the occasion, naming it the Cameneum. When Daniel Webster made his last visit to Portsmouth in 1844, it was here that he met his friends for a social evening. The Cameneum fell into disuse after the Temple became popular, and is now converted into a stable.

Mason House.

Built by Col. John Tufton Mason, fifth descendant from John Mason, original grantee of the province, semetime previous to 1746. It had originally a fine front yard, extending as far as Congress street, the grounds belonging to it reached to Hanover and High streets. Col. Mason held by inheritance the title to the whole of New Hampshire until, in 1746, he sold it to twelve individuals. This house was elegantly fitted up, and had tapestried walls, the first decorations of the kind used in Portsmouth. It only remained in the family until 1766, when it was sold.

Johnson House.

Built about 1770 by Col. Joshua Wentworth, and occupied by him for many years, before he built his house on Middle street on the spot where Henry H. Ladd now resides. He was colonel of the first N. H. regiment in 1776. He was in Congress for some years, and in 1791 was appointed by Washington, Supervisor for New Hampshire. The house was finely built, with a beautiful garden in front. It has remained ever since without material alteration, and the paper now on the parlor walls was put on when the house was built.

Assembly House.

Built by Michael Whidden about 1750, and used for nearly a century as a dancing and music hall, and sometimes for church services. Washington, who attended a splendid ball given here in his honor in 1789, pronounced it one of the finest halls he had seen in the country. It is now divided into two dwelling houses, which stand on each side of the entrance to Raitt's Court.

Meserve House.

Built in 1760 by Michael Whidden, and occupied by George Meserve, son of Col. Nathaniel Meserve. *(See Boyd estate.)* In 1765 Meserve was appointed stamp agent for New Hampshire. He was in England at the time, but on returning to this country he found the excitement regarding the Stamp Act so intense that he at once resigned the office. On his arrival in Portsmouth, however, his action on the subject not being known, he was burnt in effigy on the Parade, and obliged to make a public resignation. When his commission arrived, he gave it up to the populace, who burnt it on Liberty Bridge, (q. v.) The old oaken chest curiously carved, and with a ponderous lock occupying the whole lid, in which the stamps were enclosed, is still in existence, in the possession of J. J. Pickering.

This house was subsequently occupied by James Sheafe, who married one of Meserve's daughters ; by Dr. N. A. Haven until his house on High street was built ; by Jeremiah Mason from 1800 to 1808 ; by Daniel Webster when first married ; by Gen. Timothy Upham, and others. Two sassafras trees on the grounds are said to be as old as the house.

Drown House.

The residence of Rev. Samuel Drown, who was invited here from Rhode Island, in 1761, to be the first minister of the Independent Congregational Society, which had recently built a meeting house on Pitt street. *(See Unitarian Chapel.)* He was a faithful pastor of this society, until his death in 1770. He was the grandfather of the blind poet, Daniel P. Drown.

Treat's Marble Works.

Nearly a century ago this place was occupied by a Mr. Marble, a stone cutter, although marble was not then used as a material for grave stones. The business was purchased by Samuel Treat, who afterward removed it to Deer street, where Willow Cottage now stands. His grandson, John S. Treat, has returned to the original locality.

Haven House.

Built about 1800 by Dr. N. A. Haven, a son of Dr. Samuel Haven. He graduated at Harvard College in 1779, and was for several years a physician, and afterward a merchant. He was a warm patriot, and at one time represented the State in Congress. The site of this house is part of the original Mason estate, (q. v.) The old Pilgrim oak, on the premises, is the oldest memento of by-gone times in the city: there being sufficient reason to believe that it was a grown tree before the white men visited our shores, and is probably as old as the Boston Elm, which was blown down recently. It is now a mere ruin, but is carefully preserved. •

Webster House.

We know nothing of this old house, except that Daniel Webster lived here from 1813 to 1817. He came to Portsmouth in 1808, and resided first in the

Meserve house; then in one on Pleasant street, opposite the Jenness house, which was burnt in the fire of 1813; then in this one, where he remained until he left Portsmouth for Boston.

Fitch House.

The residence of Rev. Jabez Fitch, minister of the North Church from 1725 till his death in 1746. He was the successor of Rev. Nathaniel Rogers. Mr. Fitch was a literary man as well as an excellent pastor. He wrote a history of New Hampshire, which was never printed, but has been of great value to subsequent historians who have had access to it.

The house was afterward owned by Mr. Simeon Stiles, and is often called the Stiles house.

Vaughan House.

The former residence of George Vaughan, grandson of Richard Cutt who lived in the Great House. Vaughan was Lieutenant Governor of New Hampshire from 1715 to 1717, when he was superseded in the office by John Wentworth. When this house was built is not known, but in 1698 Mr. Vaughan was living here, and hither he brought his bride, the sister of Gov. Belcher of Maine. In 1703, his son William was born here, who was the projector of the Louisburg expedition in 1745. The tombstones of Gov. Vaughan's mother and wife are to be seen at Point of Graves.

From the Lieut. Governor all the Vaughan family in this city are descended. There is some reason to think that this old house was the residence of Richard Cutt himself, as early as 1675.

Hart House.

Built in 1737 by Capt. John Collings; it remains almost unchanged after being in the family for five generations. The parlor was handsomely finished by Cæsar, one of Capt. Collings' house slaves. Much of the original furniture remains in the house. It was for many years the abode of the venerable Richard Hart, and afterwards of Oliver W. Penhallow, who married one of Mr. Hart's daughters.

Jenness House.

Built by Daniel Hart, a brother of Richard. It was occupied as a boarding house by Mrs. Shortridge at the time of the Revolution, and here the French officers boarded when the fleet was in our harbor in 1782.

Eastern Depot.

The railroad from Boston was the first one with which Portsmouth was connected. It was completed between the two cities in 1840, and extended to Portland in 1842. The Dover Railroad was opened in 1873. The present depot was built in 1863, taking the place of the first wooden one. The site was formerly occupied by two ropewalks, erected before the Revolution, both of which remained in use until after the war of 1812, and one much longer. The latter was owned by John Underwood, who lived close by, at Underwood's corner. It was here that the ropes were made for the seventy-four gun ship Washington—its huge cable being carried down to the wharf by a procession of eighty sailors.

Livius House.

Built by Michael Whidden about the year 1750. Mr. Whidden was its first occupant, and was succeeded by Peter Livius when he left the Boyd estate, (q. v.) The house was known in his time as the White House. Mr. Livius resided here in some state, keeping three slaves; but being an earnest tory, he was obliged to leave town at the time of the Revolution; his goods were confiscated, and after he had fled to Canada, his family had to receive an especial permit from government to follow him. The house then passed into the possession of Capt. Thomas Martin, a connexion of Mrs. Livius and grandfather of the late Arabella Rice. In his day the garden walks are said to have been "paved with rare and beautiful pebbles brought from foreign climes."

Concord Depot.

The Portsmouth & Concord Railroad was open to Epping in 1848, and completed in 1852. The spot where the depot stands was formerly occupied by an old, black Distillery, and where the car house is, was a windmill for grinding bark.

Walk Seventh.

Market, Bow and Daniel Streets.

Leaving Market Square, you turn toward the North to traverse Market street. In old times it was not so designated. Among some historical memoranda left by the grandfather of Dr. Peirce, stands this one against the date of Oct. 8, 1787: "Began paving the street that leads from the Parade to Spring Hill;" the street having then no especial name; but this being the first pavement laid in town, it was afterward known as Paved street; while from Spring Hill to the ferry was called Fore street. At the time of the Revolution the aspect of the neighborhood was as different as possible from the present. The whole eastern side of the street, as far back as Chapel and Bow streets, was occupied by orchards and gardens, with a few mansions scattered here and there, while Paved street itself was no wider than Ladd street is now. On the site of the Mechanics & Traders Bank stood Mr. Dearborn's house* and school. None of the houses then standing exist at present, having been swept away in the fire of 1802; but after passing Bow street you see some old houses, though the front of one of them has been altered for business purposes. The first is the handsome Ladd house,* then follow one formerly belonging to Noah Parker,* and the old Sam. Sheafe house.* The fire spared these three dwellings, the last one burnt on this side of the street being the Sam. Cutts house.*

As you pass the foot of Deer street you see to the right the landing for the Shoals steamers. Soon after, you come to Russell and to Green streets. On the high land between these two, stood a windmill for grinding grain, which survived the other structures of the kind in town, and is still well remembered. A year or two ago Green street cemetery* would have been one of the first places for an antiquarian to visit, but now only its location can be shown. Opposite the foot of Green street was the old Ferry-way*—and just beyond stands the Stone Store.* The street ends at the bridge leading to Noble's Island, and to Portsmouth Bridge.*

Instead of going all the way down Market street, you may turn off to the right, down the street appropriately named Bow. Spring Hill and Spring Market* lie to the left, as you ascend the slope leading to St. John's Church,* and the churchyard* belonging to it.

On this commanding site, named Church Hill, a redoubt was built in the spring of 1776; and as you stand on the river bank between the shabby houses, you see how fitting a place it is for defence of the river. It is a pity that these beautiful shores should not be devoted to handsome residences, instead of sordid tenements, shops and gas works.

A few steps farther lead you round into Daniel street, at whose foot is the Navy Yard landing, from which the little steamer Emerald plies back and forth to the Yard.

The lowest part of this street, and the southern side as far as Penhallow street, were destroyed in the fire of 1813, so that nothing of interest remains; but fortunately the northern side was spared. At the corner of Bow street stands Judge Sherburne's house,* then the beautiful Warner house;* the High School building* next, and looking up Linden street, you see the old Jaffrey house,* with its noble front yard cut up into house lots. Stoodley's Hotel,* the Elijah Hall house, succeeds. To the left, on the west corner of Chapel street is the Maffitt house;* on the corner of Penhallow street, the old Post office, and opposite, the Hart house.*

Here the fire of 1813 stopped; but as far as this came an earlier conflagration in 1802, the Hart house being spared by both. Nothing of antiquarian interest remains, therefore, until you regain Market street; but many of the Sons of Portsmouth will look with pleasant memories at the house where Mrs. Massey lived, and at the door which led to her wonderful toy shop, now numbered 22.

Daniel street was opened from Market street to the

river in 1700. In that year widow Bridget Graffort, daughter of Richard Cutt, left in her will to the town of Portsmouth a highway from the Fort at Strawberry Bank, through her grounds to the river. It was called at first Graffort's lane, and afterward Daniel street in honor of Thomas Daniel. (*See High School.*)

Dearborn House.

This house, which was burnt in the fire of 1802, was built in 1750 by an English gentleman named Robinson. He was the father of Molly Driscoll, who died in our almshouse in 1835, aged 92 years. Her unhappy story is told in the Rambles. In 1780 and the succeeding years the house was owned by Benjamin Dearborn, the inventor of Dearborn's Patent Balances, as well known in their day as Fairbanks' are now. He kept a private school for both boys and girls, being the first to which girls were admitted. His pupils numbered at times as many as 120, so that he finally built an addition to his house, which served as an Academy. Mr. Dearborn afterward removed to Boston, his departure being considered a public loss.

Ladd House.

Built about 1760 by John Moffat, for his son, Samuel, who married a daughter of Col. John Tufton Mason. John Moffatt was born in England in 1692. He was a rich merchant, and married a grand-daughter of President Cutt. He lived to the age of 94.— Samuel Moffatt having failed in business, his father moved into the house himself, and Gen. Wm. Whipple, who had married his daughter, resided with him. Gen. Whipple, who was born in 1730, was one of the signers of the Declaration of Independence, member of the first N. H. Council, and General of one of the N. H. brigades. He died here in 1785. The magnificent horse-chestnut tree still standing in the yard was planted by his hand.

After his death, his widow, Madam Whipple, resided here for many years. The house afterward passed into the possession of her neice, wife of Dr. N. A. Haven, and thence to Dr. Haven's daughter, who married Alexander Ladd. It is a beautiful and spacious edifice, with a hall of uncommon elegance, and contains many valuable portraits.

Gen. Whipple had two slaves, Prince and Cuffee, almost as well known in Portsmouth as their master. After his death they lived in a small house in High street, on land given them by Madam Whipple, at the foot of her garden. Prince's widow resided here till 1832.

Noah Parker's House.

We know nothing of this house previous to the time when Rev. Noah Parker, the first Universalist minister in Portsmouth, moved into it, after selling his house on Ark street. (*See Hart house.*) He died here in 1787, and his widow kept a boarding house here after his death.

Sheafe House.

Formerly occupied and probably built by Thomas

Sheafe, son of Jacob Sheafe. (*See Episcopal chapel.*) In July, 1798, a ship from Martinique, belonging to Mr. Sheafe, discharged her cargo at Sheafe's wharf, nearly opposite the house. The yellow fever was on board, and the infection spread into the family of the owner and among the laborers. Mr. Sheafe himself lost three children, and the disease made terrible ravages in the town. During August and September there were 96 cases of yellow fever, of which 55 proved fatal. Many families left town. A guard was kept around the infected district, and all who died were buried in one common grave in the North Burying Ground. It was the only pestilence which has ever visited our city.

After the death of Thomas Sheafe, in 1831, his son Samuel resided in the same house until his death in 1857.

Capt. Sam. Cutts House.

Samuel Cutts, a direct descendant of Robert Cutt, *(see Whipple Garrison house,)* was a rich merchant and ship owner at the time of the Revolution. His wharf was opposite this house, where a row of stores now stands. It was to Capt. Cutts that Paul Revere brought a letter of warning from the Boston patriots. (*See Fort Constitution.*) In 1776 he was a member of the N. H. Assembly, and was one of a committee of three appointed to draw up the N. H. Declaration of Independence. This Declaration, adopted June 15, 1776, is a noble document, setting forth the sentiments of our state with regard to liberty, and instructing our delegates to the Continental Congress, to join with the other Colonies in proclaiming the country free.

Green Street Cemetery.

Among the first settlers in Portsmouth were three brothers from Wales named Cutt. When New Hampshire became a separate province, in 1679, one of them, John Cutt, was appointed President by the King. He and his brother Richard were the largest land owners in Portsmouth, holding all that now forms the compact part of the city. The site of President Cutt's house is not exactly known, but it was near the Ladd house—probably about where the stone store now stands. A well, discovered in 1858 beneath Market street, probably belonged to the Cutt house before the street was opened.

Green street runs through what was President Cutt's orchard, and here the family cemetery was situated, where the President and his relatives were buried. Within the last year the remains have been removed to a lot in the Proprietors' Burying Ground, where the monuments are carefully preserved.

North Ferry.

Before the building of Portsmouth Bridge in 1822, there was a regular ferry, running from the wharf at the foot of Market street to Rice's wharf at the end of what is called Love Lane in Kittery. This ferry was obtained as town property in 1722, and let out

by lease. Adams, in his Annals of Portsmouth, says
that the right of ferriage had been claimed by the
town previous to this time, but that there was no legal
grant. This year they sued for, and obtained the
ferry from government. After the building of the
bridge, the ferry was discontinued, the town paying
the lessee $4,000 for his loss. The ferry way was
kept open for Kittery boats for many years, but has
now fallen into disuse, and been built over.

Stone Store.

As nearly as can be determined, this was the site of
President Cutt's house. Here stood also at the time
of the Revolution, the Custom House and Post Office,
kept by Eleazer Russell from 1778 till his death in
1798. For some years this was the only post office in
New Hampshire. Russell was not called Collector,
but Naval Officer; but he performed the duties of
both Collector and Postmaster. The land opposite
his house, between Russell and Green streets, was
his orchard, and Russell street perpetuates his name.

Portsmouth Bridge.

Built in 1822. The first part, i. e., the bridge to
Noble's Island, is free, the main part to Kittery is a
toll bridge. Each part is provided with a draw to al-
low vessels to pass. The whole is 2,000 feet long,
the cost of its erection being $30,000. The water at
its deepest part is 53 feet deep at low tide. Many of
the craft used on the river are constructed with lat-
teen sails; so that, having a short mast, with an

exceedingly long yard, they can spread a great extent of canvas, and yet can pass freely under the bridge. These picturesque boats are a noted feature of our river, this being the only place in America where this rig is used. The Railroad bridge, which was built in 1842 close by the side of the Portsmouth Bridge, has been a great disadvantage to it, as it is now dangerous to drive a team over it when the trains are near, and it is much less used than it would otherwise be.

Spring Market.

This place has been called Spring Hill from the earliest time, receiving its name from the unfailing spring of fresh water that flows at its foot, and which was formerly covered by the river at every high tide.

In 1761 the town built a house for a market on Spring hill, one story high, which building was afterward renewed. Although other markets, more conveniently situated for many purposes, have superseded this, yet it has always remained the chief fish market. In former times it was the great resort for country traders from Kittery and Eliot, women rowing across the river in their own boats, with loads of fruit, vegetables, and all kinds of farm produce.—"The Kittery fleet" was regularly expected, and some of the women were as well known as any of the magnates of Portsmouth.

St. John's Church.

As we have seen, *(see J. K. Pickering's House,)* the first church in Portsmouth was Episcopalian, and no doubt a majority of the early settlers belonged to the Church of England. But this was not the faith of the colonies generally, and both public sentiment and the influence of government were against it. Within a year or two after his settlement, Rev. Richard Gibson was summoned to the General Court in Massachusetts to answer for some alleged offence, and never returned. No one was settled in his place, though there was preaching by various ministers. Opinion gradually changed, and by the time the meeting-house at the mill dam was built, in 1657, we find the town ready to settle a Puritan minister, although numerous proofs exist that there was still a strong Episcopal element remaining.

No Episcopal society, however, was collected until 1732, when the first church was built upon this site, and named Queen's Chapel, after Queen Caroline. She furnished the books for the pulpit, two mahogany chairs, and the plate : all of which are still in use, the flagons bearing the royal arms. The beautiful marble font belonging to the church, was taken from the French at the capture of Senegal, in 1755, by Col. Mason, and presented to Queen's Chapel by his daughters, in 1761. The bell was brought from Louisburg in 1745.

Dr. Benjamin Franklin was one of the first proprietors of this church. Washington attended service here during his visit in 1789. The first rector of the church was Rev. Arthur Brown, who officiated until his death in 1773. During the Revolution no regular services were held here.

The old church, which was of wood, was burnt in the fire of 1806, and in 1808 the present one was built. Rev. Charles Burroughs, D.D., was rector here from 1812 to 1857.

St. John's Churchyard.

Occupied as a cemetery as early as 1732. Here are the remains of many colonial governors and councillors. In the centre of the yard is a large tomb, called the Governors' Tomb, where were buried the two first governors Wentworth, with their families. The ground is so high that most of the tombs open upon the street. When the old wall was taken down and the present one built, about 25 years ago, these tombs were opened. They were quite large and full, some containing the remains of more than 100 persons. Here lie the families of the Atkinsons, Sherburnes, Jaffreys, Gardiners, and many other honored names.

Judge Sherburne's House.

John S. Sherburne, a descendant of Henry Sherburne (see *Sherburne House, Christian Shore,*) was born in 1720. He filled many public offices under the British Government, and was Judge of Probate for many years, losing his office at the time of the Revolution. He was a warm friend of liberty. This house was built by him, and after his death, in 1797, his son John resided here until he built the house No. 18 Court street, to which he removed.

Warner House.

This is the oldest edifice of brick in Portsmouth. It was built in 1718–23, at an expense of 6,000 pounds, by Capt. Archibald Macpheadris, a rich merchant and member of the King's Council. He was a native of Scotland, an enterprising man, and the chief proprietor of the Iron Works at Dover, the first iron works established in America. He married a daughter of the first Governor Wentworth, and died in 1729. The huge elk antlers that still hang in the hall were given to Capt. Macpheadris by his friends the Indians. His daughter Mary married Jonathan Warner in 1754, and from the latter the house takes its name. Mr. Warner was also a member of the Royal Council until the Revolution. He lived here until a good old age, but leaving no children the house passed into possession of his great-nephew, Col. John N. Sherburne, a cousin of Judge Sherburne.

The brick for the construction of this house was brought from Scotland—the original bills for the materials are still in possession of the family. It is an elegant specimen of the architecture of the last century, and is rich in memorials of old times. The frescoes in the great hall are by the hand of an unknown artist; and having been papered over, were forgotten for generations, being accidentally discovered about twenty years ago. The lightning rod, probably the first in New Hampshire, was put up in 1762 by Dr. Franklin. The odd little house a short distance from the front door, at the corner of Sheafe and Chapel streets, stood formerly adjacent to the mansion, being the slave quarters.

High School.

Built in 1858 for the two High Schools, which at that time were distinct. In 1873 the schools for boys and girls were united into one.

The spot where this building stands was formerly occupied by an old house resembling the Warner House, built by Thomas Daniel, a merchant, about 1680. Thomas Daniel married Bridget Cutt, a daughter of Richard Cutt; who after his death married Thomas Graffort, in 1684, and in her will bequeathed this street to the town. At the time of the Revolution this house was inhabited by Mark Hunking Wentworth, a distinguished merchant. He was the father of Gov. John Wentworth, who lived on Pleasant street, but unlike him was a patriot. He died here in 1785.

Jaffrey House.

Built probably as early as 1730 by George Jaffrey 2d, (*see Jaffrey house, Newcastle,*) then Treasurer of the Province of New Hampshire and Chief Justice of the Supreme Court. His son of the same name resided here until his death in 1802. He also was Treasurer of the Province until the Revolution. He was strongly opposed to the change of government, remaining a tory until his death. Having no children, Mr. Jaffrey intended to leave his large property to Col. Joshua Wentworth, (*see Johnson house,*) but becoming offended with that gentleman, he left it to his great-nephew, George Jaffrey Jeffries, of Boston, on condition that he should drop the name of Jeffries, and never follow any profession but that of a gentleman; which conditions were accepted. The last George Jaffrey died in 1856. Francis W. Ham has in his possession an old clock, which was in the Jaffrey family from the year 1677, and is still in order. This mansion and extensive grounds were elegantly kept by their former owners; the handsome porch and magnificent linden tree on the premises still attract many admirers.

Stoodley's Hotel.

Built soon after 1761 by Col. James Stoodley, and kept by him as a tavern, replacing one which was burnt in that year. It was the most fashionable hotel in Portsmouth, and the usual stopping place for travellers between Boston and Maine. The upper story, with its lutheran windows, was all one arched hall, used for dancing parties and for Masonic purposes. After Col. Stoodley's death, his widow was married again to Mr. McHurd, but still kept boarders here. The house afterward came into possession of Hon. Elijah Hall, who married Col. Stoodley's daughter, and who died here in a good old age.

Maffit House.

Here resided the famous Methodist preacher and revivalist, John N. Maffit. He was the first minister

stationed here after the building of the Methodist
Church on State street in 1828.   At that time his son
John, afterwards so widely known as the commander
of the rebel privateer Florida, was about 10 years old.

Hart House.

Built about 1740, but it is not known by whom.
When the first Stoodley tavern was burnt, in 1761,
this house was much injured, and Wyzeman Clagett,
who was living here, removed, in consequence, to the
house in Congress street.   (*See Miss Leavitt's house.*)
At the time of the Revolution, Noah Parker lived
here, and it is said the house was called from him
Noah's ark, which gave its name to Ark street, now
Penhallow.   In 1791, Jacob Sheafe bought the place,
and gave it to his daughter Hannah, wife of Hugh
Henderson.   After Mr. Henderson's death, his widow
married William Hart, and continued to reside there,
keeping a small shop where Gilbert's store is now.
She died in 1845, at the age of 99.   The street opposite, the northern part of Penhallow street, was not
opened until the present century.

Walk Eighth.

Elm Street. Christian Shore.

If from the Eastern Depot you turn to the north-west and go through Elm street you have an interesting walk before you. You pass the North Cemetery* with its row of old poplars,* then the Raynes house* and shipyard, then the North Mills* and Mill Bridge. Beyond the bridge lies Christian Shore,* through which North street leads. Notice the ancient tannery on the right as you pass; and crossing Dearborn street, which would only lead to another tannery, turn to the right, when you reach the Hay-scales down a little oblique lane. It is worth following, for it leads into an odd little nook of old buildings, and turning to the left it passes the most ancient of all our houses, the Jackson house.* The path comes out upon Cutts' Hill, where there is a pleasant view, and into North street again near the Franklin school. At the corner of Prospect street stands the old Jones' homestead, and if you go a little way down this street past two or three old dwellings, you come to the Dennett house,* most royally situated of yore on a terraced hill.

Pursuing your way through North street, you pass the Cutts house ;* and going on in the same direction out of town, you reach Hon. Frank Jones' farm, Mark H. Wentworth's farm* and Newington. If you turn to the right, at the Cutts house, you will arrive at Freeman's Point.*

Instead of following North street so far, if you take the left hand on reaching the Hayscales, you go through Dennett street. At its entrance stands the old Timothy Ham house,* and then you pass a row of tenements built on the Dennett house terraces, the mansion looking down over their heads. After a while, the road divides into Woodbury and Myrtle streets ; and here, across the fields, you see the Sherburne House.* Myrtle street will lead to the Almshouse, and out to Creek street. Woodbury street, once the pretty Jericho lane, lined with barberry bushes, leads you along the shore of the North Pond, past some old houses, near one very ancient red one, and then through a suburb laid out within a few years. It was hoped by the projectors, that if streets were opened the wealthy inhabitants of the city might be attracted hither, but the railroad and the breweries were too near. This street also ends in Creek street, just beyond the Woodbury mansion.

North Cemetery.

This lot of land was sold to the town in 1753, for a

cemetery, by Col. John Hart. Interments had previously been made here, although the Point of Graves had been the principal burial place. Land to the north and west of the original acre was afterwards purchased by the town from Dr. William Cutter. The place contains many interesting mementos, among them the marble monument brought from England by Col. Boyd in 1787 The colonel died on the voyage, and the monument was at once erected.

The oldest inscriptions now legible are those of Jotham Odiorne, (who married a daughter of Robert Cutt,) 1751, renewed by his descendants, the Treadwells; Dr. Benjamin Dearborn, 1755; Sarah Hart, 1757; and Richard Wibird, 1765. There are also the tombs of Gen. Wm. Whipple, Col. Joseph Whipple, and their sisters Mrs. Trail and Mrs. Brackett; Eleazer Russell, Drs. Clement and Hall Jackson, J. M. Sewell, Sheriff Packer, Master Toppan; and of many of the most distinguished Portsmouth families, such as the Buckminsters, Goddards, Sheafes, Moffats and Mannings.

Poplars.

These trees are the last remains of the many rows of poplars that decorated our streets some eighty years ago. The first were set out by Hon. John Langdon, in front of his residence on Pleasant street, in 1792. They soon became the rage, and Pleasant, Deer, Jaffrey and Broad streets were bordered with them, beside other places. .Rev. Mr. Alden, in his century sermon, congratulates the people of Portsmouth on these ornaments, and hopes that "so laudable an example will be followed, until every vacant street and corner shall be furnished with the Lombardy poplar."

The trees soon lost their beauty, however, and went out of fashion as rapidly as they had come in, giving place to a generation of buttonwood trees. These, too, soon lost favor, and were replaced by the maples and elms which now beautify our streets.

Raynes House. (Boyd Estate.)

Built about 1740 by Col. Nathaniel Meserve, a ship builder and colonel in the British army at the siege of Louisburg in 1745. In 1749 he built for the government, a man-of-war of 50 guns, in his shipyard which was situated near the present one. He commanded the New Hampshire forces in the Crown Point expedition of 1756. In 1758 he went to the second siege of Louisburg, where he died.

After Col. Meserve's death the house passed into the hands of Peter Livius, who was born in England in 1727. He there married a daughter of John Tufton Mason of this town, who was finishing her education in England, came here with her in 1762, and resided for several years in this house.

About 1768 Col. George Boyd purchased the place and considerably enlarged it. This gentleman had become suddenly rich, (*see Rock Pasture*,) and lived in magnificent style. His garden extended to the present site of the Eastern depot, and was elegantly laid out; at intervals, handsome posts were erected, surmounted by carved grenadiers' heads. The house with its numerous outbuildings was called the White Village; and the Mill pond was named Boyd's Creek. During the Revolution Col. Boyd, though not calling himself a tory, retired to England. On his return in 1787, he died at sea, two days before the ship reached land. His son William succeeded him in the possession of the estate. In later years it passed into the ownership of George Raynes, and the old Meserve shipyard again became the scene of activity. Here Raynes built between 60 and 70 vessels, the largest being little short of 2000 tons. The yard is now awaiting a new revival of shipbuilding among us.

North Mills and Bridge.

In 1764 Peter Livius, then residing on the Boyd estate, made proposals to the town, to build a bridge across Islington Creek, on condition that the exclusive right to dam the stream and use it for mill purposes should be secured to him. This was agreed to. The bridge was to be 20 feet wide, with a portion 30 feet long to be a "lifting bridge" for the passage of vessels; the whole to be toll free. The North' Mills were built at the same time, and called Livius' Mills, which name they long retained.

Christian Shore.

The origin of this name is uncertain, but tradition ascribes it to some families of strictly Puritan principles who resided here in the earliest times. There were but few houses built here before the construction of the bridge. This place is sometimes called North Portsmouth.

Jackson House.

This is probably the oldest house in the city, and is an interesting relic of colonial architecture. It was built in 1664 by Richard Jackson, who owned land in the vicinity, amounting to 26 acres. It still belongs to the descendants of the original owner. The house fronts on the river, as all the oldest houses did, being built at a time when the river and the different creeks were the chief highways, the shore being covered with an almost continuous forest.

Dennett House.

The date of the building of this fine old mansion is uncertain, but it is said to have been the second house built on the Shore. The lower part is constructed throughout of solid square timbers. The terraced grounds in front extended as far as the river, and it must have presented a fine appearance when it stood alone on the hill. It is probable that it was built by an ancestor of the Dennett family, as the name has always been associated with it. Ephraim Dennett, who married Lydia, a daughter of Timothy Waterhouse, (see *Timothy Ham house*,) lived here at the time of the Revolution. His widow afterward married Judge Plummer of Rochester. The house is known in the neighborhood by the cognomen of the Beehive.

Cutts' House.

Built about 1810 by Edward Cutts, a son of Capt.
Samuel Cutts, *(see Samuel Cutts' House,)* and a merchant of high standing in Portsmouth. The grounds
were laid out in beautiful style, and the orchards were
filled with remarkably fine fruit. Mr. Cutts' son
Hampden resided here after his father's death, until
1833, when he left town, and the house was sold.

Mark H. Wentworth's Farm.

To reach this beautiful River-side estate you turn off
from the Newington road just beyond the Jones farm.
It was originally owned by President John Cutt, *(see
Green Street Cemetery,)* and in his will, dated 1680,
it is left to his son Samuel; being described as "my
land near the Pulpit, by the water side, being 70 pole
in breadth, and running up the whole length into the
woods." A subsequent clause provides that his beloved wife Ursula (his second wife) should have the
use of the land during her life, if she should choose
to live there. The President died the next year, and
his widow went to reside at the Pulpit farm, where
she made many improvements, and on which she lived in a style of great elegance for thirteen years.

In the summer of 1694, an attack was made by the
Indians upon the place, and Madam Cutt was murdered by them, together with three men who were
busy in her mowing fields. The only other woman
on the place, Madam Cutt's maid, escaped in a boat
over to Ham's Point, (now Freeman's,) and thence to

Portsmouth, where she gave the alarm, but the Indians were not overtaken.

The farm remained in the Cutt family until it was bought by Hon. Ichabod Bartlett, from whom it passed to the present owner. The name of Pulpit farm was derived from a well known rock on the river bank, called the Pulpit.

Freeman's Point.

Formerly called Ham's Point. This picturesque point of land was one of the first places in the vicinity that was settled. In 1652 a grant of fifty acres was made to William Ham, and in 1654 another grant was made to Matthew Ham of "a lot next his father's new dwelling house." A year or two after, he received 25 acres more, so that all the Point belonged to the family. It remained in their possession until the present century. The site of the Ham mansion, and of the family burying ground are still shown.

Timothy Ham House.

About the year 1700, Timothy Waterhouse, a grandson of William Ham, built a house near the old mansion on Freeman's Point, where the cellar may yet be seen. The house itself was moved hither more than a century ago, and remodelled into the present dwelling by Timothy Ham, great grandfather of F. W. Ham. The builder, Waterhouse, was a farmer and tanner. One of his grandsons, Dr. Benjamin Waterhouse, a professor in Cambridge, was the first to introduce vaccination into this country. The first operation was performed on his own son, in 1800.

Sherburne House.

Built by Samuel Sherburne, who died in 1765. The ancestor of the Sherburne families in this vicinity, Henry Sherburne, came to Piscataqua among the first settlers in 1631. He was church warden in 1640, of the first Episcopal chapel, which, as one of his descendants spicily remarks, "was broken up by the Bay puritans; the document about which is the only thing left of our early town records, which were burnt by the Bay puritans in the civil wars, when they re-annexed Maine and New Hampshire to their empire." The name appears in all our early history. Henry Sherburne 2d (*see Portsmouth Pier*) was one of the councillors of the Province; his son, born in 1709, was also named Henry, and was a brother of Samuel, who built this house. The estate has remained in the family until within a few years.

Places in the Immediate Vicinity.

To a pedestrian of average ability, many places of interest in our neighborhood lie within easy reach, and the drives around Portsmouth are noted for their variety and beauty.

To give directions to all such places, outside of the town, as a visitor would wish to find, would be almost impossible in a volume so concise as this is intended to be; nor is it needed, as information can be easily obtained. All that will be attempted therefore, is briefly to describe the chief localities of historical interest in the immediate vicinity, though, as the preface states, the list is by no means complete.

Odiorne's Point, though at some little distance, is first mentioned, as being the earliest historical landmark. The other places, that follow, are arranged chiefly by neighborhoods. The Shoals have already a literature of their own, and no allusion has been attempted either to Rye, Hampton or York, as it would lead us farther than our plan contemplates.

Odiorne's Point.

Capt. John Mason, a merchant of London, was one of the first who took an interest in colonizing New England. He was secretary of a council established in Devon, by royal charter, for planting and governing New England; and from this council he obtained for himself and Sir Ferdinando Gorges, in August 1622, a grant of land comprising all that is now New Hampshire. To this land they gave the name of Laconia; and, with other merchants, they formed the so-called Company of Laconia. In May 1623, this company sent out the first settlers of New Hampshire, under the leadership of a Scotchman named David Thompson, who landed at the mouth of the Piscataqua. Part of the company went about eight miles up the river and established themselves on a neck of land now included in Dover. The rest settled on Odiorne's Point and built a Manor House, afterward called Mason Hall. In the document setting forth the claim of Robert Mason to New Hampshire, written 1679, this house is described as "a very fair and large house of stone and timber, by him called Mason Hall, encompassed with a ditch and strong palisades, and fortified with eight guns," within it being "arms and ammunition and other necessaries for the defence and protection of the inhabitants." About 1000 acres of meadow ground were improved at the same time. The site of Mason Hall is yet to be seen, also the old well belonging to it, the cemetery and the site of the smith's shop. The cemetery is well preserved, the old part being filled by about forty graves, which have rough head and foot stones, though no names are preserved.

As early as 1660 this point of land was in possession of John Odiorne, who gave his name to it. It has ever since remained in the family. A movement has been recently begun to erect a suitable monument on this interesting spot, and preparations for it are being made.

New Castle.

In the document above referred to, it is stated that "said John Mason did build many houses upon the great island that lieth at the mouth of said river Piscataway, upon which he erected a fort, and mounted it with ten guns for the defence of said island and river." This island, ever since called Great Island, was then considered as a part of Portsmouth; but in 1693 it was incorporated under its present name of New Castle. In these early times it was of equal importance with Portsmouth, and its history, which we cannot now enter into in detail, deserves to be fully written. Some of the family names here are as ancient as any in the country, though few sites can be definitely located; the Waltons, the Amazeens, the Atkinsons, the Jaffreys, Sheafes, Frosts and Lears have left records in our history, and many of the most eminent citizens of Portsmouth trace their origin to New Castle. The Provincial governors resided here for years, and the commerce of the place was extensive. It is now of less comparative importance, but is exceedingly interesting to visit.

For many years there was no connexion except by water between New Castle and the main land. In 1776 it was voted in the N. H. Legislature to build a bridge or bridges in order "to secure a retreat for our forces to be stationed at New Castle, in case of a defeat;" but there is no record that this purpose was ever carried out.

In 1801 a bridge was built connecting Great Island with Rye, but after about twenty years it fell into disuse and decay. In 1822 the present bridges were built, uniting it with Portsmouth by the way of Shapley's and Amazeen's Islands; the whole length of the bridges being 2371 feet. In 1874, when the hotel named The Wentworth was erected, another bridge was built to the main land at the mouth of Sagamore Creek, often called Davis' Point.

Fort Constitution.

As we have already seen, a fort was built by the very first colonists upon Great Island. The location was called Fort Point, and has ever since been used for the same purpose. The first fort was an "earthwork, with certain great guns." In 1666 a more regular fortification was built, and Richard Cutt was appointed Captain; who was succeeded by Elias Stilesman, and, in Cranfield's time, by Walter Barefoote. William and Mary became sovereigns of England in

1689, and about that time the fort was named after them, being called indifferently the Castle or the Fort William and Mary. It was always considered a place of importance, although, no regular sum being appropriated for its preservation, it was continually falling into ruin, and needing repairs. When the Revolutionary troubles began, John Cochran was commander of the fort. In Dec. 13, 1774, "one Paul Revere arrived express with letters from some of the leaders in Boston to Mr. Samuel Cutts," bringing reports that troops were embarking at Boston to take possession of Fort William and Mary. Great excitement prevailed, and the following night a body of men under Capt. Thomas Pickering went down to New Castle, seized the fort, hauled down the King's colors, and carried off 100 barrels of powder, which they stored under the old South Church. Part of this powder was afterwards used at Bunker Hill. Returning the following night, the patriots carried away all the light artillery; and would have entirely dismantled the fort, had not Gov. Wentworth written to Gen. Gage for assistance, who sent two men-of-war in time to prevent it. During the summer of 1775, the British themselves dismantled the fort, and the Committee of Safety taking charge of it, placed it under the command of Gen. Sullivan. It was at first named Fort Hancock, then Fort Constitution. In the next year an attempt was made to recover the cannon "carried by the King's Ships from our

Castle to Boston and probably left there;" but they could not be found.

In the war of 1812 it was kept fully garrisoned, under Capt. Marshall, who commanded here for several years.

During the Mexican war the garrison was removed, and the fort remained unoccupied except during a brief period, until the time of the southern rebellion. In 1863 new and extensive fortifications were commenced here, but they have never been completed, and probably never will be.

Light-House at New Castle.

Built by Gov. John Wentworth in 1771. As early as 1765, while Benning Wentworth was Governor, a petition was presented by sundry inhabitants of Portsmouth setting forth the necessity of a light-house at some suitable place near the mouth of Piscataqua Harbor. A committee was appointed to examine the matter, and a sum was appropriated for the erection of such a building, but being entirely insufficient, nothing more was done. In April 1771, Gov. John Wentworth made an earnest appeal to the Provincial Assembly to have enough appropriated to keep at least a lantern lighted at the head of the mast that supports the flagstaff in the Castle, or Fort, saying in this appeal: "Every future expiring Cry of a drowning Mariner upon our coast, will bitterly accuse the unfeeling Recusant that wastes that Life to save a paltry unblessed Shilling." A sum was accordingly granted; but in December of the same year, the governor announced that having found this mode of lighting impracticable, he had himself exceeded the grant, and caused the needed edifice to be erected. The debt thus incurred was paid the next year. In 1789 the light-house was ceded by the State to the United States. In 1854 it was remodelled and cut down, in order to distinguish it from the light-house on Whalesback.

Jerry's Point.

The point of land thus named (a corruption from Jaffrey's Point,) was fortified very early, probably soon after Fort Point, though we have only tradition for our authority. The same tradition states that the brass guns for the battery were provided by the merchants of London. The ancient earth-works on the north-east side, consisting of three rude but heavy walls inclosing about one-fourth of an acre, and six small parapets, remained plainly visible until 1873. At that time they were needlessly destroyed by the government officials, when the present works were commenced. During the Revolution, barracks were erected here, and the place was fully garrisoned; but after the peace, the cannon were removed to Fort Constitution and the land given up to its owners. During the war of 1812, two other small earth-works were erected, and were used for a short time. These also have been destroyed, but with reason, as they were on the site of the new works. These latter, when completed, will mount eight guns.

Jaffrey House. (Mr. Albee's.)

Built by the first George Jaffrey, who was born in Newbury in 1637 and removed to Newcastle in 1677. This house was built previous to 1680. Gov. Cranfield, during his oppressive administration, from 1682 to 1685, ejected Mr. Jaffrey from his house, which he occupied himself, and here the Provincial Council was more than once held.

George Jaffrey 2d was born here in 1683 but removed to Portsmouth prior to 1719. (*See Jaffrey House, Daniel street.*) Here Theodore Atkinson resided for a time, before his removal to Portsmouth. (*See Atkinson House.*)

During the last war with England, Col. Walbach, who commanded at Fort Constitution, lived here. The house is beautifully situated, is in fine preservation, and is one of the most interesting in our vicinity.

Walbach's Tower.

Built in Sept. 1814, when an attack by the British upon New Castle was hourly expected. Col. Walbach, then in command of the Fort, summoned the inhabitants to the aid of the garrison, and this tower was constructed with great speed. Not being found necessary, it was neglected, and soon assumed its present ruinous appearance.

Sheafe House.

The house which stands at the parting of the roads to the Fort and to the Wentworth, is held to be their ancestral house, by tradition in the Sheafe family; and is sufficiently venerable to warrant the belief.

The first of the name in this part of the country was Sampson Sheafe, who came to Newcastle in 1675, and passed several years here, residing at other times in Boston. He was Collector of Customs, and member of his Majesty's Council. His son Sampson was born here in 1681; he held the office of Councillor for over 20 years. His son Jacob was born here in 1715, but in 1732 removed to Portsmouth. (*See Episcopal Chapel.*)

We have noticed but one or two of the places of interest in New Castle; but the visitor there will find many others. The gambrel-roof cottage, for instance, which stands near the Post office, on Cold Fox Point, so called, is known to have been the residence of Allen, boatswain to John Paul Jones in all his memorable cruises; and of later interest is the carriage house, once a school house, which the Freewill Baptists point out as the place where Randall, the founder of their sect, preached his first sermon.

Wentworth House. Little Harbor.

One of the best known and most visited of the historical places in our neighborhood. The house was built in 1750, by Gov. Benning Wentworth, who resided here until his death in 1770. He was appointed Governor of New Hampshire in 1741, at the time of the final separation of this state from Massachusetts, and his rather stormy administration continued until 1766, when he was succeeded by his nephew, John Wentworth.

In 1755, being left a widower, he married his house-maid, Martha Hilton, the heroine of Longfellow's poem of "Lady Wentworth." At his death, he left the estate to her, and she soon afterward married Col. Michael Wentworth, an English officer, not related to her first husband. Col. Wentworth had seen good service in Europe, having been engaged in 1745 at the battle of Culloden, under the Duke of Cumberland, and at the battle of Fontenoy in France, in 1746.

During Washington's visit to Portsmouth in 1789, Col. Wentworth entertained him at his residence. In 1800 John Wentworth, a grandson of Mark Hunking, married the Colonel's daughter Martha, and resided here until they went to Europe in 1816. The estate was then purchased by Charles Cushing, who married a daughter of Jacob Sheafe, and in whose family it still remains. This house originally contained 52 rooms, but a portion having been removed, the number is now reduced to 45. The parlor, the council chamber with its old portraits, and the billiard room, are shown to visitors upon the payment of a trifling fee. The chimney piece in the council chamber, before which the Governor stood to be married to his maid, was carved with a knife and chisel, occupying the workman more than a year. Among the portraits is one by Copley, of Dorothy Quincy, afterward Madam Hancock : one of Secretary Waldron, and one of Sir Thomas Wentworth, Earl of Strafford, after Vandyck. The cellarage of the house is very extensive, and was arranged for the stabling of 30 horses in time of danger.

Sagamore Creek.

This beautiful inlet, formerly called Witch Creek, received its present name from the Indian chief or Sagamore, said by tradition to have once resided upon its banks.

The earliest English settler on the Creek was Ambrose Gibbons, a steward of Mason, the founder of the colony. In 1622 Mason had founded another colony, at Cape Ann, of which Gibbons was agent until 1630, when the Massachusetts Bay Company "violently seized upon that part of the province," and turned out the servants of Mason, "upon pretence of a charter from King Charles in 1628." Gibbons then came and settled here, and when Francis Williams was chosen governor of the plantation in 1640, he became assistant Governor. His daughter married Henry Sherburne. *(See Sherburne House.)* His farm was afterward named Sanders' or Sandy's Point, from one of his descendants.

Though this creek was settled early, it has never become a seat of business, and has remained much as it was 200 years ago. From its present aspect, with dwellings scattered here and there, and portions of the primeval forest still standing, we can recall to our imaginations the earliest appearance of Portsmouth itself. The Mill Ponds, and even Puddle Dock, were inlets like this, and the Great House stood among such woods.

Near the mouth of the Creek is the picturesque cottage of T. S. Coffin ; and a little further up is the old Martine farm, which has been in the family for many generations. The house is very old ; perhaps it was built by Richard Martine, whose name appears in the church record of 1693.

Here Estwick Evans, the "pedestrious traveller," and poet was born. Here Louis Philippe passed a week during his visit to Portsmouth in 1798 ; and some flowers from the garden sent to him while on the throne of France, by one of the family, were acknowledged in an autograph letter. The farm was purchased from the family by Franklin Pierce, and used by the ex-President for some years as a summer residence.

The southern side of the Creek, at its mouth, was occupied, until within a few years, by the Sheafe farm ; through which land the new road to New Castle now runs. On the same side also is the small farm owned by Benjamin Lear, known as the Hermit. Here he lived alone in a hut for more than twenty years, denying himself the common comforts of life ; and here he died in 1802, aged 82 years. His mother had previously died in the same hut, at the great age of 102. Mr. Lear never would speak of Portsmouth except as the Bank.

Among the Sagamore woods is a precipice of moderate altitude known as the Lover's Leap, from which, according to tradition, a deserted Indian maiden threw herself.

Sagamore bridge was built in 1850, when the road was opened through to Rye. The house so finely situated at the head of the bridge, was built by Abner Greenleaf, the first mayor of Portsmouth.

Elwyn Farm.

Tobias Langdon, a grandson of Ambrose Gibbons, was born on the farm at Sagamore in 1660. In 1687 he settled on this farm, which has ever since remained in the family. John Langdon, the grandson of Tobias, who was afterwards Governor, (*see Governor Langdon's House,*) was born here in 1739. His only child, Elizabeth, married Thomas Elwyn, and their son was John Elwyn, the late owner of the place. He was born in 1801 in England, where his parents were travelling, but resided in Portsmouth until his death in 1876. He was a gentleman of some eccentricities, but a scholar of great acquirements, especially in history and philology.

Elwyn Park.

In 1867 John Elwyn gave about five acres of land, lying on the south side of the South Mill Pond, to trustees for a public Park, to be laid out as such, at any time when they should deem it best. So quietly was the gift made, that, until the donor's decease, it was almost unknown to the public, and no steps were taken toward carrying out the plan proposed; but as these pages go to press, the project has been revived, and the Park has been commenced in good earnest.

Langdon Farm House.

Built about 1700 by Capt. Samuel Banfield, whose name is perpetuated in that of a road close by. He died in 1743, and the place came into possession of Joseph Langdon, who had married a daughter of Capt. Banfield. It has always remained in the family. Part of the house shows its great age, but part has been modernized. Near the dwelling is the burial place, with a handsome monument bearing the family records. The farm itself is extensive, containing 120 acres.

Warren Farm House.

Built about 1740 by Col. Thomas Westbrook, whose daughter was the wife of Secretary Richard Waldron.

Richard Waldron was born in the year 1694; he was the son of Col. Richard Waldron, who succeeded John Cutt as President of New Hampshire. When an infant, he narrowly escaped death by the hands of the Indians, together with his father and mother; a mere accident having prevented their visiting Madam Ursula Cutt on the day of the massacre. (*See Wentworth Farm.*) He fixed his residence at first on the ancestral estate at Dover, but afterwards removed to Portsmouth, and lived at the Plains. In 1728 he was appointed Councillor, and soon afterwards Secretary of the Province. In 1745 his house at the Plains burnt down, the public records being lost in the conflagration; after which time he resided in this house, which was built in the best style of those times. He died in 1753. The house afterwards passed into the possession of the Moffat family. (*See Ladd House.*) It has never been modernized, and is fast falling to decay.

The Plains.

At the time of the first settlement of the province, quite a village was built in this neighborhood, and here was made the most murderous attack by the Indians that our local history records. On the morning of June 26, 1696, the savages fell upon the little settlement, burned five houses and nine barns, and killed fourteen people. Several others were wounded, and still others made prisoners; but most of the inhabitants succeeded in reaching the garrison-house, after a desperate struggle. This garrison-house stood in a field north of the present school-house.

Among those wounded and left for dead was Mrs. Mary Brewster, who afterwards recovered, and became the mother of several children, from whom are descended the Brewster family in Portsmouth.

The village was not abandoned, but increased; and in 1725 we find the inhabitants numerous enough to build a meeting-house for themselves "at vast expense." It did not stand long, however, for in 1748 it was taken down, and the worshippers re-united themselves with Dr. Langdon's parish.

The only road from Portsmouth to the Plains was then a very circuitous one, through Frenchman's

Lane; the direct road from the Creek was not opened until 1792; Middle road, leading past the old Pound, being laid out about the same time.

The Plains have always been in favor as a place for military exercises and reviews. In the days of slavery in New England, Portsmouth had her share of black chattels; in 1727 there were 52 owned here. These slaves had every year a mock election at the Plains, choosing a king, amid great festivities.

Breakfast Hill.

As soon as the attack by the Indians upon the Plains, in 1696, was known in Portsmouth, a company of militia, under Capt. Shackford, set out to intercept them in their retreat. They overtook the savages while breakfasting upon this hill, with their captives in their midst. The soldiers fell upon them, and recovered the prisoners and the plunder, but the Indians escaped. The hill took its name from this affair. The three tall pines on its summit, are the shattered remains of a group of six, which was a landmark from the sea for generations.

Greenland.

The name of Greenland dates back to the earliest settlements, though until 1705 it was considered as a part of Portsmouth. The road leading to it through Great Swamp, was opened in 1663; this was the direct road to Boston, and of course a very important thoroughfare. At the time of the great prevalence of small pox in Boston, in 1764, a fence was built across this road by the Portsmouth selectmen, and a house erected in which all travellers from the former city were smoked, together with their luggage; and an office near the Pound was established in other years for a similar purpose.

Greenland contains many beautiful farms, and the rides through it are charming. In the last century it was as pleasant and flourishing as now. In the letters of the Marquis de Chastelleux written from Portsmouth in 1782, he says, "We passed through Greenland, a very populous township, composed of well built houses. Cattle here are very abundant. The country presents, in every respect, the picture of abundance and happiness."

Peirce Farm.

About 1640, Francis Champernowne, (*see Gerrish's Island,*) purchased 400 acres of land in Greenland, which included part of this farm. He built a house here, in which he resided for nearly twenty years, returning afterward to his abode at the Island. He bought about 200 acres more, while in Greenland. His estate here afterward passed into the possession of Col. Packer; and when Greenland was divided from Portsmouth in 1705, its boundaries were fixed "at the south side of Col. Packer's farm." It apparently remained in the Packer family until 1809, when it was purchased by John Peirce.

The first of the name of Peirce in this country was Daniel, who settled in Watertown, Mass., in 1634. His grandson, Joshua, came to Portsmouth about 1700, and married Elizabeth Hall, a granddaughter of John Hall. He, by this marriage, acquired part of the Hall property, to which his grandson, John, added the adjoining Packer Farm. *(See Peirce House,)*

March Farm.

About the year 1663 the land of this farm was granted by the crown to John Hall, who settled here. One of his grand-daughters married Israel March, who came from Massachusetts about 1700; and in this branch of the family the farm has ever since remained. His son, Clement, who was born in 1707, added greatly to its extent. Col. March was commander of the Horse Guards under Governor Benning Wentworth, and was also Judge of the Court. He was the representative of Greenland in General Court for twenty years or more, and was a man of great influence. He was succeeded in the ownership of the estate by his son, Dr. Clement March, a physician, grandfather of the present owner.

Robert Weeks Farm.

The old brick house standing on this farm is probably the most ancient in New England. It was built about 1638 by the father of Leonard Weeks, who was in 1662 one of the Selectmen of Portsmouth. The

bricks of which it is built were burned in front of the
house.   It was evidently intended for a garrison
house, being constructed in the. strongest manner;
the walls are 18 inches thick, and the beams in the
cellar 12x14.   The windows are of small diamond-
shaped panes.   The house bears marks of having
been injured by an earthquake, probably that of
1755, when, on Nov. 18th, "a most severe and tre-
mendous earthquake" took place, shocks being felt
every day for a fortnight afterwards.

The lane on which this house stands was part of
the first road opened through the woods to Portsmouth.

Newington.

The first name given to this point of land was
Bloody Point, on account of a quarrel about its possession, between Walter Neal, the agent of Gorges
and Mason at Piscataqua, and Capt. Wiggins, agent
of the company at Dover.   Though no actual hostil-
ities took place, the name commemorated what
might have been.   It was retained until 1713, when
the inhabitants of the village petitioned the General
Assembly that they might be made a distinct parish
from Portsmouth and Dover.   Their petition was
granted, on condition that "they forthwith establish
an able, orthodox and learned minister among them."
The name of Newington was given at that time, but
the old designation still clings to the extreme point of

land where the railroad to Dover crosses the river. On this land stands the old farm house, famous for drop cakes, known as "Nancy Drew's" to every Son of Portsmouth.

Rollins Farm.

This farm, which has been in the same family for six generations, was originally owned by James Rawlins, (the same name as Rollins,) who came to America in 1632 with the Ipswich settlers. He came to this place, then considered as a part of Dover, in 1644, receiving a grant of land. In 1656 another lot of 100 acres was granted to him here. Whether Rawlins himself, or one of his sons, built the house now standing, is not known, but the oldest part of the house is of great antiquity. It has been much enlarged, but the four original rooms are retained. The splendid Rollins Elm, near the house, is probably as old as the first settlement of the place. Its trunk at the smallest part, is 22 feet in circumference.

Pickering Farm.

In 1655 the town granted John Pickering 1st, (*see South Mill*,) a lot of land lying on Great Bay; and in 1660, fifty acres more were added. John Pickering himself lived in Portsmouth, on Pickering's Neck, (*see Pleasant Street*,) and was buried at Point of Graves. He was one of the most influential of the early settlers, and his posterity retained much of his firm and energetic character. He left two sons, John,

who inherited Pickering's Neck, and Thomas, who
took the land in Newington. Thomas' first son,
James, born about 1680, was a lieutenant in the
French war, and from him and his brother Joshua,
almost all the Pickering families in Greenland and
Newington have descended. The beautifully situated ancestral farm is retained in the family; and the
old house, built by the first Thomas, stands yet,
though it has been altered so many times that nothing remains of the original four-roomed structure,
but the frame, which is made of oak as sturdy as its
builders themselves.

Piscataqua River.

The first voyager who visited the Piscataqua, as far
as we know, was Martin Pring, who came to the
shores of New England in 1603, with about fifty men,
in two vessels, the Speedwell and the Discoverer.
They were sent out by the city of Bristol, in England, to make discoveries on our coast. They visited
the rivers of Maine, and then entered the mouth of
the Piscataqua, which Pring calls the westernmost
and best river, ascending it for ten or twelve miles.
He speaks with admiration of the goodly groves and
woods upon its banks.

In 1614, the river was visited by Capt. John Smith,
who gave New England its name. Smith was so
much pleased with the place that he probably influ-
enced his friend, Sir Ferdinando Gorges, in his selec-
tion of it as suitable for his colony.

The river and harbor were called by the Indians Piscataquack, which after various changes by the early settlers, has softened into Piscataqua. It is a peculiar river, being rather an inlet of the sea, into which flow the united waters of several small rivers, of which the principal are the Cocheco and Salmon Falls. The current is very deep and rapid, so that it never freezes over, and forms one of the best harbors in America. The tide rises about eight feet, and flows up as far as Dover. A sail up the river, amid the beautiful and varied scenery, is a delightful excursion for a summer's day.

Piscataqua Bridge.

Built in 1794 by a company incorporated for the purpose. It was a great undertaking, as the river is generally upward of fifty feet deep at the place selected, and the bridge was over 2000 feet in length. The cost was $62,000, part of which was raised by a lottery. It was expected to be of essential benefit to Portsmouth, but it proved to be too far up the river, and after the building of Portsmouth Bridge, in 1822, it fell into disuse and decay, and was finally swept away by the ice in 1840. The old tavern beside it, which had been for years a great resort of pleasure parties, also fell to ruins, but the neighborhood is still visited by all lovers of river scenery.

Islands in the Harbor.

Piscataqua river joins the ocean two or three miles below Portsmouth, enclosing several islands. These are divided by the State line into such as belong respectively to Maine and New Hampshire. The Maine islands are, as you descend the river, Badger's, the Navy Yard, Seavey's and Gerrish's Islands. The New Hampshire islands are Pierce's, Shapley's, Goat, Pest, Marston's or Salter's, and Leach's Islands, beside the rock at the mouth of the harbor on which stands Whalesback Light house.

Of the Navy Yard and Gerrish's island we shall speak separately.

Badger's Island was formerly owned by Gov. Langdon, and was called by his name. When the Revolution began, and the Continental Congress was looking out for some place to begin to build a navy of its own, Langdon offered them the use of this island. It was accepted, and in March 1775, the frigate Raleigh was begun. In sixty days she was launched, and Capt. Thompson, (*see Dwight House*,) took command of her.

In 1776 Congress ordered three ships of 74 guns to be built or purchased. Only one was built, the America; the heaviest ship that had been constructed in this country. It was commenced on this island, but the necessary funds failed, and when John Paul Jones was ordered here in 1779 to take command of her, he found that she was not half built. For three years he watched over her, until her completion; when she was presented by the government to France as compensation for the Magnifique, lost by accident in Boston Harbor. She was a splendid vessel. In later times William Badger had his ship-yard here, in which he built one hundred ships, nam-ing the hundredth for himself.

Seavey's or Trefethen's Island is separated from Peirce's by the passage called the Narrows, through which the tide runs with great violence. It has re-cently been purchased by the United States as an ad-dition to the Navy yard.

During the Revolution a fort was built and gar-risoned on this island, and called Fort Sullivan. In 1863 a company of contrabands was stationed here, for military drill and for protection to the harbor if needed

Peirce's Island belonged originally to Dr. Renald Fernald, the surgeon sent over by Mason with his col-ony. Dr. Fernald is the ancestor of the various fam-ilies of the name in Portsmouth. A. R. H. Fernald, a direct descendant, has in his possession a chair brought over by the doctor. In 1688 the island was owned and occupied by Richard Waterhouse, a tanner, who married one of Fernald's daughters. In the summer of 1775 batteries were built on this island, as well as on Seavey's; "several hundreds of men from the country round, voluntarily laboring thereon." The fort in this place was named Fort Washington, and the island bore for a time the name of the Isle of

Washington. This fort and fort Sullivan were both
under the command of Capt. Titus Salter, a brave
and energetic officer, who resided in the house noticed in our first Walk, (page 7,) which was built
for his father. They were of great importance, and
did much for the protection of the harbor and town
from the destruction which was continually threat-
ened by the British Navy. After the peace, the cannon from these two forts were removed to Fort Point,
and the barracks were sold. In 1812, they were
rebuilt and garrisoned for awhile. The earthworks
are still to be seen. The island has occasionally
been used for shipbuilding.

Shapley's Island was occupied a hundred years ago
by a hospital for small-pox patients. Before the dis-
covery of vaccination, parties were wont to be formed, called small-pox parties, which all who wished
to be safe from the natural form of the disease,
joined, and all were inoculated at once. These parties, strange to say, were made the occasion of social
gatherings, and were attended with much festivity.

In 1822 the bridges to New Castle were built,
which connect this island with the main land and with
Goat Island, and Goat Island, which is quite small,
with Great Island.

Pest Island is so named from the hospital which is
situated there for small-pox and other contagious
diseases; the hospital on Shapley's Island having
been taken down when the bridges were built.

The group of rocky islets at the mouth of the harbor, on one of which stand the U. S. Quarantine buildings, are called Wood Islands and Fishing Islands; they are famous places for boating parties. On another rock stands Whale's Back Light-house, built about 1825. In 1873 the second tower was erected, and the first is now used only for storage purposes.

Salter's or Marston's Island is the one which presents so picturesque an appearance from the South road and Little Harbor road. It is cultivated as a a farm, and has one house upon it. A bridge connects it with the mainland.

Navy Yard.

The island on which the Navy Yard now stands, and Seavey's Island, were granted under the name of Puddington's Islands, by Sir Ferdinando Gorges to Thomas Fernald, a son of Dr. Renald Fernald. They were to descend in the family by entail, "as long as the grass grows and the water runs," but when the right of entail was abolished by the State of Maine, they passed out of the family. This island was still called Fernald's, and was used for drying fish, having only one house upon it, until 1800, when it was purchased by the United States for a Navy Yard. Up to this year, the island known as Badger's (q. v.) had been used virtually as a Navy Yard. At this yard some of the finest vessels in the American Navy have been built, of which we will only mention the

Kearsarge, which sunk the Alabama. The yard is pleasantly and conveniently situated, and is an interesting place to visit. There are three ship houses upon it, one of which contains the unfinished iron-clad, Massachusetts. In the centre of the Yard stands the Office Building. The other buildings interesting to strangers are the Ordnance Building, near the Gun Park, the Machine Shop, the Boat Shop, the Pattern Shops, and the Saw Mill. The floating dry dock attracts the eye at once, lying as it does near the landing, from which the small government steamer makes several trips a day to the foot of Daniel street.

Gerrish's Island (or Gerrish's and Cutts' Islands.)

In the year 1636 Sir Ferdinando Gorges gave two large tracts of land in New England to the brother of his second wife, a gentleman of Devon named Arthur Champernowne. The family of Champernowne was among the highest in England, being allied to the Plantagenets. Sir Walter Raleigh and Sir Humphrey Gilbert were connected with the family.

Arthur Champernowne seems to have transferred the grant in New England at once to his son Francis, born in 1614, who came to take possession of the place at once, in 1636. One of the tracts of land lay in what is now York; the other consisted of this island, then considered as two islands. Here Francis Champernowne resided, except during the years he spent at Greenland, until his death in 1687. The islands were to have taken the name of Dartington, after the paternal estate in England, but they were popularly known as Champernowne's Islands, a name they should have retained. Francis Champernowne lived in baronial style both here and at Greenland, and filled the highest offices. He was a Councillor in the Gorges' government of the province as early as 1641; in 1665 he was appointed one of the Royal Commissioners to govern the State of Maine. In 1684 he became one of Cranfield's councillors in New Hampshire, and at the time of his death he was councillor to Sir Edmund Andros. His character was worthy of his high position. His tomb has no monument but a cairn of stones; tradition says that this was by his own request. About ten years before his death he married the widow of Robert Cutt, and leaving no children, the island passed into the possession of the Cutts family, and afterward into that of the Gerrish family, who still own it.

The island is divided nearly in two by what was formerly called Braveboat Harbor or Creek; now known as Chauncey's Creek, sometimes as Brawboat Creek. It is connected with Kittery, to which it belongs, by a bridge, which in Champernowne's time was a drawbridge, raised every night for protection from the Indians. The road through the island is rather lonely and rough, but commands lovely sea views, and the antiquarian will find two houses of extreme age, the Cutts' farm house, said to be 230 years old, and the Gerrish house, which claims to be older.

Kittery and Kittery Point,

The first settlements made in Kittery were as early as 1623 under Walter Neal, the agent of Mason and Gorges. It was at first called Piscataqua, but in 1641 it was incorporated under the title of Kittery, a name taken from that of a little English hamlet, though it was often called Piscataqua, even to the time of Pepperell. Hubbard, in his History of the Indian Wars, written 1676, says, "on each side of that brave, navigable river of Piscataqua, down toward the mouth of it, are seated on the north side the town of Kittery, a long, scattering plantation, made up of several hamlets, and on the south side the town of Portsmouth." Kittery then comprised North and South Berwick and Eliot, as well as Kittery Foreside, Kittery Point, and Gerrish's Island, which now compose it. In 1646 it paid nearly half of the taxes of Maine; and Josselyn mentions it as the most populous of all the plantations of Maine. It affords most delightful and picturesque views, and contains many old houses and sites of interest. Kittery Point is a peninsula, approached by a short toll-bridge over Spruce Creek, or by a circuitous route through York.

Adams Farm.

This pleasantly located farm, whose buildings attract the eye as you approach Kittery over Portsmouth Bridge, was in the Adams family for more than 200 years. An old deed in possession of Capt. Samuel Adams, dated 1664, sets forth how Jeremiah Shoores and Susanna his wife, have, " for a certain sum of money," sold to Nathaniel ffryor, of Portsmouth, in Piscataqua, 100 acres of land on the north side of Piscataqua river, allowed and granted to him by the town of Kittery. Another deed, dated 1668, conveys the same from Nathaniel ffryor to Christopher Adams, "marynor," for eighty pounds. Mark Adams, great-grandson of Christopher, was for more than twenty years representative of Kittery in the Maine legislature. Every Sunday he used to scull across the river to attend Dr. Buckminster's church. The old mansion house stood until within twenty years.

Whipple Garrison House.

This old house, situated on Whipple's Cove, so called, was built for a garrison house at a very early date, though the precise year is not known. Until recently altered, it was a fine specimen of the architecture of such houses—with the upper story projecting over the lower, so that the doors and windows could be protected from the Indians, and with very small, strongly defended windows. It was probably built by the inhabitants of the little hamlet in the neighborhood. Later it became the residence of Robert Cutt 2d. The first Robert Cutt a brother of John and Richard, lived at first in the Great House, and then removed to Kittery to carry on his business of shipbuilding, which was very extensive. His widow married Francis Champernowne. His son Robert, who lived in this house, had four daughters, one of whom married William Whipple, Sen. William Whipple, her son, born here in 1730, became Gen. Whipple, the signer of the Declaration of Independence. When he married his cousin, Catherine Moffatt, he went to live at the house of her father on Market street. *(See Ladd House.)*

Rice Farm.

This estate was granted by Sir Ferdinando Gorges to a family by the name of Withers, and in 1652 it was given as a marriage dowry by Thomas Withers to his daughter Mary, who married Thomas Rice. It has remained ever since in the Rice family, and seven generations lie in the family lot on the old farm. Near by this lot grows a rosebush known to be over two hundred years of age.

On this farm was the landing place for the ferry from Portsmouth, *(see Ferry Ways,)* long known as Rice's Ferry; and through the woods passed the old road to Portland. Part of this road has been always called Love Lane, from its beauty and seclusion, apparently, though now but few traces of either remain. The old Rice mansion stands near the ferry.

Kittery Point Church.

Built in 1714. The frame was cut in Dover, and floated down hither. The plate that belongs to the church was a bequest from the elder Pepperell. The building has been recently moved and turned around to the south.

This was not the first meeting house built in Kittery: one was erected in 1699, under the ministry of Rev. John Newmarch. In the old cemetery opposite the church can be found many interesting memorials and some old epitaphs, among them the well known one :

I lost my life on the raging seas,
A sovereign God does as he please;
The Kittery friends they did appear,
And my remains they buried here.

Pepperell House.

Col. William Pepperell, the father of the baronet, came to this country in 1676, and resided for several years at the Shoals, where his son was born. He afterward removed to Kittery Point, where he became an eminent merchant and shipbuilder, dying in 1733. This old mansion was built by him and his son sometime before his death.

Sir William was born in 1696, and resided here until his death in 1759. This "Piscataquay trader," as Smollett calls him, was the first American baronet, being knighted for his services at the capture of Louisburg in 1745. His possessions were very extensive, reaching as far as the Saco river, where he owned 5000 acres, the site of the present town of Saco. This family mansion was then much more imposing than at present, being ten feet longer at each end, and surrounded with a beautiful park, well stocked with deer, and extending to the river. A fine avenue of trees led from it to the residence of Col. Sparhawk. Sir William's only son Andrew having died in 1751, the baronet adopted his grandson, William Sparhawk, as the heir to his title and estate, on his taking the name of Pepperell. At the time of the Revolution, young Sir William, being a tory, took refuge in England, taking his grandfather's rich plate with him; and in 1779 the estate here was confiscated, except a widow's dower reserved to Lady Pepperell, and $30,000 dollars given to Mrs. Sparhawk for her interest in her father's property.

Pepperell Tomb.

Built in 1733, at the death of the elder Pepperell. It became very much out of repair in the course of years, but was put in order by the last descendant of the family in this country, Harriet Hurst Sparhawk. The scattered bones were collected into a crypt built in a corner of the tomb. The remains of about thirty bodies were found.

Bray House.

Called in the neighborhood, Settler Bray's house; one of the oldest buildings remaining in the country. It was built about 1660; its name being taken from John Bray, a ship builder, father of Margery Bray, the wife of the elder Pepperell and mother of the Baronet. It was formerly much larger than now, the back part with a sloping roof, extending far toward what is now the main road. The visitor to this house and the Pepperell mansion, should remember that when they were built, the road had no existence, the houses being approached from the river, toward which they front. Of course they are not now seen to advantage. In one of the rooms of this house is an old picture, representing the siege of Louisburg, painted on a panel over the fireplace. The windows and banisters show extreme age. Near by the house, at the waterside, may be seen the ruins of the old wharf, where Mr. Bray and the Pepperells conducted their large business.

Cutts House.

Built by Lady Pepperell after the death of Sir William in 1759. She left the old mansion when this one was completed, and resided here until her death in 1789. The house then came into the possession of Capt. Joseph Cutts, who was born in 1764, being a direct descendant of Robert Cutt. Captain Cutts was ruined by the war of 1812, and became insane; two of his sons were also insane. His daughter, Sally, took the whole charge of her father and brothers for many years, until, worn out by trouble, she too lost her reason. After the death of the others, Sally Cutts lived here alone until a short time before her own death, which took place in 1874. The house since then has been thoroughly repaired.

Sparhawk House.

Built by Col. Nathaniel Sparhawk, who married Elizabeth, only daughter of Sir Wm. Pepperell, in 1742.

The first Nathaniel Sparhawk came from England in 1640, and resided in Cambridge. His grandson, the Colonel, went into business in Boston, but upon his marriage with Lady Elizabeth, came and settled here. He was a man of influence, and held many public offices. This house was very handsomely built, and its various rooms were hung with differently colored damask, red, blue, yellow, each room taking its name therefrom, after the English fashion. Elizabeth's father sent to England for her wedding dress, which was to be "of white padusoy silk, flowered with all sorts of colors suitable for a young woman." Col. Sparhawk died in 1789, and his widow went to Boston; but one of his sons, Nathaniel, came back to the family mansion in 1809, and died here in 1815, when it was sold.

Fort McClary.

As early as 1700 a fort was erected on this site, and in 1714 the elder Pepperell was chosen captain of the garrison. It was called from him Fort Pepperell, but since the Revolution it has received the name of McClary in remembrance of one of New Hampshire's most gallant sons. Andrew McClary, born at Epsom, N. H., was major of the 1st New Hampshire

Regiment, under Gen. Stark. He was tall and of fine personal appearance; said by one of his fellow officers to be the handsomest man in the army.

He fought bravely at Bunker Hill, and was killed after the battle by a chance shot from one of the ships of war, as he returned from examining the position of the enemy.

The fort was repaired and the block house built in 1845–6. The extensive works, now half completed, and destined never to be finished, were commenced during the Rebellion, at the same time as those at Fort Constitution.

INDEX.

The places mentioned in the Index are only those which are separately described, and to which an Asterisk is affixed in the Walks.

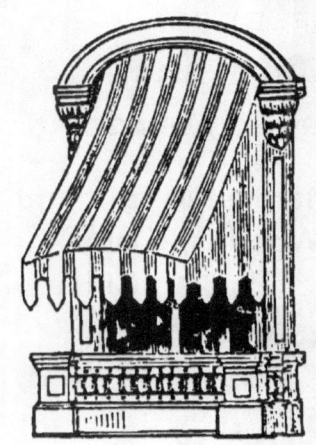

PEPPERRELL HOTEL

KITTERY POINT, ME.

E. F. SAFFORD, PROPRIETOR.

This Hotel has been in successful operation for four seasons, under the management of its present proprietor.

It is a popular, healthy and quiet resort, delightfully cool during the summer months, with pleasant surroundings and good facilities for boating, fishing and bathing.

It is three and a half miles from Portsmouth, N. H. and is reached by a regular stage line from Portsmouth and Kittery Depots, which runs twice each way daily.

KITTERY POINT STAGE.

The Stage makes two trips each way daily; connecting at Portsmouth with trains to and from Boston, Concord and Dover; and at the Point with the Seaside houses.

The route leads by the old Pepperrell and Sparhawk Houses and affords fine views of the Navy Yard, River and Harbor.

THEODORE KEEN, Proprietor.

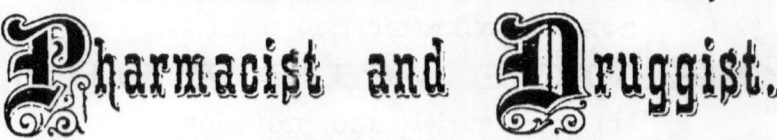

www.ingramcontent.com/pod-product-compliance
Lightning Source LLC
Chambersburg PA
CBHW031118020726
47495CB00007B/2258